LOVE AND LIES

When Dana Abraham agrees to look after her friend's secretarial agency, she must deal with Alexander Mitchell, who has rejected every woman the agency has sent: the prettier they are, the meaner he is. Dana decides to fulfil the role of perfect secretary herself, and goes in a frumpy disguise to win him over. But Mr Mean-and-Moody Mitchell is not the bully she expects, and she finds herself becoming attracted to him. It seems he has growing feelings for her, too — but will they last when he discovers her deception?

PAMELA FUDGE

LOVE
AND LIES

Complete and Unabridged

LINFORD
Leicester

First published in Great Britain

First Linford Edition
published 2016

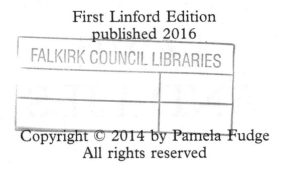

Copyright © 2014 by Pamela Fudge

A catalogue record for this book is available
from the British Library.

ISBN 978–1–4448–2944–0

Published by
F. A. Thorpe (Publishing)
Anstey, Leicestershire

Set by Words & Graphics Ltd.
Anstey, Leicestershire
Printed and bound in Great Britain by
T. J. International Ltd., Padstow, Cornwall

This book is printed on acid-free paper

1

'I can't go back. I won't go back, and — I'm sorry — but you can't make me.'

Dana Abraham flinched at the woman's vehement tone, and her heart sank. 'He can't really be that bad, surely?' She could hear a pleading note creeping into her voice and, despising herself for sounding so feeble, wondered what on earth Gillian would do in a case like this.

'He's worse, he really is.' The woman leaned forward, gripping the handbag on her lap until her knuckles showed white. She was obviously very upset.

Reminding herself that she was the one in charge here, however temporarily, Dana tried even harder not to let her own anxiety show. She sat up straighter, tucked her long dark hair behind her ears, and took a deep breath. 'All right, Jenny,' she said, keeping her voice calm and allowing no hint of criticism to surface in her tone, 'I'll sort something out.'

'I don't want to let anyone down,' Jenny said apologetically, 'but the man really *is* impossible to work for, and I'm not joking.'

Dana reached for one of the cards in front of her on the desk and placed it before the woman. 'Do you think you could manage this?'

Jenny barely glanced at it. 'After him,' she said firmly, 'anything will be a doddle.'

She left happily enough, clutching the information about her next job. But Dana, staring at her retreating back, felt as if the weight of the whole world had just descended onto her slim shoulders. She looked skywards and heaved a deep, heartfelt sigh. 'Why does this have to happen to me on my first day?' she demanded of the high ceiling. 'I'm only here to help out.'

She found that she was reaching automatically for the phone, before common sense stilled her hand on the receiver and told her to think again. She couldn't bother Gillian at a time like this, and over something that was probably quite trivial anyway. Perhaps one of the other ladies . . .

The door was pushed open and Dana looked up expectantly, part of her thinking — hoping — that it would be Jenny back to say that she had reconsidered. It was a vain hope, but she managed a smile anyway, as Gillian's assistant Kerry looked in.

'Trouble?' Kerry asked, her bright head tipped to one side enquiringly.

'You could say that,' Dana said wryly. 'It seems that Jenny has just walked out on one of Gillian's clients, and she flatly refuses to go back.'

'Alexander Mitchell?'

The question, asked in a very knowing tone, brought Dana's head up with a surprised start and she stared at the other woman. 'Do you know him then, Kerry?'

'Never actually met the man, but I do

know about his reputation.' A vigorous nod set the red bobbed hair swinging. 'And so do the ladies. Most of them have walked out on him at one time or another.'

Dana didn't know whether to be impressed or appalled. 'He's really *that* bad?' she asked.

'He's worse.'

'Oh, dear. That's what Jenny said.'

'And she was right.' Kerry sat down on the corner of the desk. 'I think we've got trouble with a capital T, Dana.'

'If he's that bad shouldn't we just tell him to get lost?'

Kerry shook her head emphatically. 'Too valuable, I'm afraid.'

'But if he's so terrible . . . ' A thought struck her suddenly. '*Why* is he so bad, anyway? Sexual harassment, throwing things . . . ? What?'

'Oh, no, nothing remotely like that,' Kerry denied at once. 'Just generally arrogant, mean, and moody as far as I can tell, but worse, if you know what I mean.' She paused for the briefest

4

second before adding, 'Especially with attractive women.'

'What?' Dana laughed disbelievingly. 'You're kidding me.'

Kerry held up one hand. 'Scout's honour.'

'You're not a scout,' Dana pointed out.

The girl grinned. 'I wanted to be, once.'

'Tell me what you know about Mr Mean-and-Moody Mitchell.' Dana put her elbows on the desk, and her chin on her hands, and looked at Kerry expectantly.

'I'll make coffee, shall I?' She stood up, adding, 'This could take some time.'

* * *

The office was quiet, the phones for once were silent, and through the window Dana could see that it was just beginning to get dark. She glanced at the clock and sighed deeply. Almost eight o'clock, and she was no nearer a solution than she had been hours ago.

She glared at the thick file on the desk in front of her and wondered in despair how one man could upset so many people. It wasn't impossible, obviously, because this Mr Mitchell seemed to have done it in a relatively short time and in such a way that women who had never met him were flatly refusing to even consider working for him. Dana wouldn't have believed it if she hadn't spent most of the day ringing anyone who was even halfway suitable.

What was she to do? She was at a complete loss. It had seemed such a simple thing when she had offered, without hesitation, to take over the running of her friend's small recruitment agency while Gillian's mother was ill. Now here she was, on her very first day, faced with the prospect of losing one of the agency's most important clients.

Something had to be done — but

what? She could hardly appeal to the man's better nature when it was painfully obvious that he didn't have one. The wonder was that he continued to deal with the same place when he found all the personnel he had been sent so far sadly lacking in some way.

Apparently, as Dana discovered from his records, he was a writer of some sort. That could explain his being a bit temperamental, she supposed, but not — if Kerry and the other ladies were to be believed — downright obnoxious. Dana tried, for the umpteenth time, to concentrate on the options that were open to her in dealing with this case. The obvious, and the simplest one, was finding the man someone else to take Jenny's place; but as Dana had discovered for herself, that was going to be all but impossible when the guy's ugly reputation had become common knowledge among the women on Gillian's books.

Another alternative that came reluctantly to mind involved her confronting the man, explaining her predicament and his, and suggesting to him that he apologise to the last woman he had upset in the hope that she might return. Dana grimaced horribly and admitted to herself that it was a silly idea, and doomed to failure anyway.

She looked at the phone longingly. It would be so simple to punch in Gillian's number, explain her problem, and ask for her advice. Then she sighed. Simple, yes, but also impossible.

She stood up, a little stiffly from the time she had spent sitting, and began to pace the room, hoping desperately that a solution would suddenly present itself — because there had to be one, surely? She remembered with a wry grimace how, so recently, she had been at great pains to assure her friend that she was leaving her beloved agency in very capable hands.

'Don't worry, Gill,' she could still hear herself saying in her own confident tone. 'I shall manage perfectly well with Kerry's help.'

She could see again the relief on her

friend's face as she had accepted her offer. 'Of course,' Gillian had said, 'Kerry knows all there is to know about the business. She can help with any problems you come across.'

'There you are, then.' Dana had patted her arm. 'Go to your mum — she needs you — and we'll keep the place running like clockwork in your absence. It's what friends are for.'

What friends are for... The words ran and reran inside Dana's head, reminding her of what a true friend Gillian had always been — and reminding her that she could not possibly let her down now, not at a time like this.

Dana's eyes grew dreamy and she forgot, for the moment, her surroundings and the problem that she faced, as she recalled the circumstances that had drawn them together all those years ago.

It was a well-known fact that opposites attract, and it was true that she and Gillian Spencer had been nothing alike in looks or nature. Dana was taller, darker, and more serious in her outlook, whereas Gillian was tiny, blonde, and bubbly. Tragedies in their lives had isolated them from their peers, and had thrown them, almost reluctantly, together. The loss of a parent would always be a cruel blow, but to have such a terrible thing happen as you teetered on the edge of womanhood was doubly devastating, and Dana sometimes felt that they had only eventually been able to cope because they had each other, and so knew someone else who really did understand. There were differences in the circumstances of the tragedies, of course — Gillian's father had died as the result of an accident at work, while Dana's mother had contracted a virus — but their deaths were both sudden and totally unexpected, and those dark days had forged a bond between the two girls that could never be broken.

'You still have a father,' the fourteen-year-old Gillian had said, 'and I still have a mother.'

Dana recalled nodding, and reminding them both, 'We're luckier than some children who have nobody.'

'In some ways it may be harder for the parent we have left,' Gillian had said, in a struggle to be fair, 'because one day we'll find love, but they've lost theirs.'

'We'll make it up to them.' Determination had crept into Dana's tone. 'In a small way. If we work hard and make them proud of us.'

*   *   *

'So that's what we did,' Dana said after she had related the whole story to Kerry the next day. 'We worked hard at college, each with the encouragement of our remaining parent. Gillian went into recruitment and eventually opened this agency, and I went into interior design.'

Kerry reached for coffee that had gone cold while she listened, and she nodded. 'It explains a lot. I always thought you were sisters, even though you don't look at all alike. Do you still have your business?'

Dana shook her head. 'I gave it up when my father got ill two years ago. He needed me, you see, and I wanted to be with him. He died a few months ago. It was Gillian who again saw me through. She made me take time out to recover before getting my life back into some kind of order.'

'I envy you two your friendship,' Kerry admitted honestly. 'It's a rare and precious thing in today's world.'

'So you must see now,' Dana almost pleaded, 'why it's so important to me that I handle this crisis without Gillian's help. She's done so much for me, and this is my chance to repay her. She doesn't need any more problems right now. With her mother fighting cancer, she has enough to worry about.'

They were both silent for a moment, each deep in thought, and then Kerry suddenly spoke. 'I'll go,' she said.

'What?' Dana stared at her uncomprehendingly. 'Go where?'

'To Mr Mean-and-Moody's.' Kerry

laughed at the shock that Dana was aware was apparent on her face. 'I *am* a secretary,' she added unnecessarily.

Dana's spirit's soared momentarily, and then plummeted as common sense took over. 'You can't,' she said flatly.

'I can.'

'No, you can't. Think about it. He hates attractive women,' she pointed out, 'and you, Kerry, are far too eye-catching.'

'I can tone down my make-up and dress down.' Kerry was enthusiastic in her effort to be of help, and Dana could have hugged her. 'I can do it.'

'I don't doubt it,' Dana agreed, 'but there's one other thing you seem to have overlooked.'

'And that is?'

'That I can't run this agency without you,' Dana reminded her. 'Basically, I'm just sitting in Gillian's chair. You're the one with the knowledge of the day-to-day running of everything.'

Kerry looked disappointed for a minute and then brightened. 'I could teach you.'

'I appreciate your confidence in me.'

Dana tried to smile. 'But I'd like Gillian to have an agency to come back to.'

They lapsed into a gloomy silence that was broken only when the phone began to ring, making them both jump.

'I'll make some more coffee,' Kerry offered as Dana's hand reached for the receiver. Picking up the used cups, she had left the room before Dana spoke into the instrument.

The very masculine voice that answered Dana's cheerful 'Can I help you?' sent shivers along her spine that seemed to start all the way down from the soles of her feet. In fact, she was so busy concentrating on the dark, velvety tones that it was a second or two before she made sense of the words that were being spoken. When she did, she found herself sitting up very straight in her chair and had to fight the urge not to actually stand to attention.

'You call yourself a secretarial agency.' The tone was deceptively silky, and icily polite. 'So is it too much to ask that you send to me one — just one — halfway

14

decent and fully trained secretary?'

It was the first customer complaint that Dana had had to deal with, and she was determined to get it right. 'I'm so sorry to hear that you haven't been satisfied with the service you've received,' she replied apologetically, 'and I will, of course, do all I can to put matters right for you.'

'Well,' the voice drawled, 'I'm pleased to hear it.'

'If you'll give me your name, and the nature of your complaint,' Dana offered, 'I'll deal with it immediately.' Her pencil was poised efficiently over the pad, and Kerry had just crept into the room with two fresh cups of coffee. Dana grimaced up at the girl and mouthed the word 'complaint', and Kerry raised her eyebrows expressively.

'A pity your staff aren't as helpful.' The man's disapproving tone grated on her, but Dana determined to keep her cool and not allow him to ruffle her feathers.

'You are . . . ?' she prompted.

'Alexander Mitchell,' he stated, as if that explained everything — as indeed it did.

The tip of Dana's pencil pressed so deeply into the paper that it left a deep, black gouge before it broke with a loud snap. 'M-Mr Mitchell.'

Was that quavering voice really her own? And did the mere mention of his name really have the power to make Kerry, with all her bright confidence, start so suddenly that she spilt hot coffee in muddy puddles on the desk? If his voice over the telephone could instil such fear, then how much worse must he be in person? Dana couldn't even begin to imagine, but she was quite sure that she didn't want to find out.

'Yes,' he said coldly.

Watching Kerry scurrying to fetch a cloth, and looking in disbelief at her own hands trembling and at the broken pencil, Dana decided there and then that *nobody* should have that much influence over people's thoughts and feelings. 'Perhaps you could tell me,' she said in a deceptively calm voice, 'exactly what's been wrong with each of the women we've sent you, because there have been rather a lot of them.'

'Certainly — if you have a few hours to spare, and a large pad to take notes.' He made no effort to disguise the sarcasm in his tone, or the irritation.

Before Dana could reply, she found she had to make a very conscious effort to control her own annoyance. She had read his file through very carefully — in fact, she seemed to have done little else since she'd arrived in the office — and from it she knew that Gillian had sent him only her very best, most efficient employees. There had been no other complaints made about the quality of their work, which did rather seem to suggest that the man was exceptionally hard to please. Either that, or he took a malicious delight in being plain awkward. She found herself nodding as if in complete agreement with her thoughts, and felt her mouth curve involuntarily. 'Perhaps just the main faults then,' she encouraged him, trying not to let the smile show in her voice.

'Suffice to say,' he snapped, 'that they were certainly more interested in their own appearance than in the presentation of my manuscripts. That apart, they were slow and uniformly inefficient — typical empty-headed females, in other words.'

Dana fumed as her temper rose, and she had to nip her tongue firmly between her teeth. For sheer arrogance, he almost took her breath away. She had a clear picture of him sitting, smug and self-satisfied, behind his desk, and she longed with all her heart to tell him just exactly what she thought of him.

She had actually opened her mouth to speak — telling herself that someone had to do it, and that someone might just as well be her — when something stopped her. No, she acknowledged — not something, but someone. Someone who deserved better from her than the behaviour she'd been about to indulge in. It *was* being indulgent, too, she reminded herself as Kerry came bustling back in to dab energetically at the rivers of coffee that ran through, and over, the paperwork on the desk.

'Are you still there? Or are you as inefficient as the staff you supply?' The questions, barked in Dana's ear, made her jump, and Kerry raised her eyebrows again and stopped dabbing for a moment.

'Oh, yes,' she assured him sweetly from between gritted teeth. 'I was just deciding how best I could deal with this to our mutual satisfaction. You obviously feel you've had poor service from us, and I would, of course, like the chance to change your opinion.'

'Well . . . ' He sounded surprised. ' . . . that's more like it. Perhaps we can still do business, after all.'

Dana scowled horribly into the receiver, and Kerry snorted before clapping her hand firmly over her mouth in case her mirth was heard over the phone. 'I'd like that,' Dana lied gallantly through her clenched teeth, and added hurriedly,

'Just tell me exactly what you look for in a good secretary, and I'll ensure that she's on your step first thing Monday morning.'

She listened carefully, murmuring assent every few seconds, and noticing that the man was turning on the charm now that he thought that he was getting his own way. The deep voice was almost soothing now that the biting sarcasm was missing, but Dana refused to be soothed. She thought that she had never been so angry in all of her twenty-six years, and only the thought of Gillian, and her good name, made her hold her tongue.

'Arrogant, conceited, pig-ignorant . . .' she grumbled after he rang off, and banged the receiver down with all the force she possessed. She would not have been surprised to see it disintegrate all over the desktop.

'Sounds familiar, and that's only for starters,' commented Kerry. 'He's obviously a complete swine *and* a male chauvinist into the bargain. So what on earth were you doing promising him another secretary?'

Dana groaned loudly and clasped her head in her hands. 'I don't know,' she admitted. 'The words were falling out of my mouth before I could stop them. It was the only way I could prevent myself from telling him where he could stick himself and his books.'

'Now what?' Even Kerry was looking worried. 'You won't let me go, and there's no one else.'

No one else. Not one person on Gillian's books who was willing to work for Mr Alexander Mitchell. Not one . . .

The answer hit her quite suddenly, right between the eyes, and when she raised her head she was smiling. 'Oh yes there is,' she said. 'There's me. I'll go.' She looked up at Kerry. 'What's the matter? Cat got your tongue?'

2

Dana found herself laughing out loud as she pictured again the look on Kerry's face when she had dropped her bombshell.

'You?' The woman had been positively spluttering. 'But — you can't.'

Dana had looked right into her startled brown eyes and demanded, 'Give me one good reason why not.'

'One?' Kerry had laughed mirthlessly. 'I could give you a dozen, and all valid.' Then, seeing that Dana was serious, she added, 'You're not even a secretary, and he's already rejected the best that Gillian had to offer.'

'I passed all the same secretarial exams Gillian did.' She held up her hand to silence further protests that were bound to be forthcoming. 'I know it was a long time ago, but I used a lot of the skills I learned for my own business. I'm sure I can do it.'

'I admire your confidence, and with anyone else I'd be right behind you in this.' Kerry shuddered graphically. 'But we're not dealing with your usual person here, are we? You know as well as I do what you'll be up against.'

'I'm all we've got left,' Dana had pointed out firmly, 'so I'll just have to do.'

Kerry was obviously struck by the plain truth of that statement, and fell silent — but only for the briefest moment before she said in a rush, 'You're much too pretty; he'll hate you. And who's going to run this place, anyway?'

'You are.'

'Me? I can't . . . You wouldn't . . . '

'You know almost as much about running this place as Gillian does,' Dana declared, 'and certainly more than I do. You run the office — get one of the ladies to help — and I'll tackle Mr Mitchell.'

'Well . . . ' Kerry looked half-impressed and half-worried. 'I'd better wish you luck then, because I know how much you're going to need it.'

* * *

Monday morning, and the smile slid from Dana's face as she recalled again the conversation, and Kerry's heartfelt wish at the end of it. She tried for a moment to convince herself that the man could not possibly be as bad as his reputation suggested. No one could really be that difficult.

Then she remembered his unpleasant manner on the phone, and she knew she was only trying to fool herself. He was that bad — probably a whole lot worse — and if he ever discovered that she was not what she was pretending to be . . . Dana shivered at the thought.

She had been so confident when she set out that morning. After a weekend spent with Kerry re-organising the office, and also time spent working on her own image, she'd been so sure that she could be what this man seemed to be looking for in a secretary. Why, even Kerry had begun to change her tune.

Dana shook herself mentally and straightened her back. It was too late to start having doubts now, when in a few more minutes she'd be facing the man himself. She had been practising the cool, calm, and collected manner for days and couldn't afford to get into a state of nerves at the eleventh hour.

Trying to quell her trepidation, she took in her surroundings as she drove down the lane, trying to appreciate the green of the countryside on the outskirts of Salisbury and imagine the type of house the wretched man called home. Probably something bold and brash; she was already imagining a disgusting blot on this beautiful landscape. Her lip curled as she pictured him playing the country squire — when he wasn't churning out his bestsellers, of course. She frowned as she realised she had no real idea of what he looked like, nor was his name familiar to her. Yet, according to Kerry, he was very well-known even outside of literary circles, and often made the gossip columns.

Of course, she thought, her brow clearing, one had to read the gossip columns or watch the television to recognise the likes of Alexander Mitchell, and she had done neither for quite some time. In the first place, she had been too busy shaping her own career; and, more recently, she had been nursing her father and had lost all interest in the outside world and the celebrities it was peopled with. She never used social media or wasted time on Google. Her laptop was, or had been, used specifically for work, and it had been gathering dust for quite some time. She only hoped her office skills hadn't been gathering dust as well.

Lost in thought, Dana almost passed the turning into a driveway so camou- flaged by vast rhododendron bushes that the entrance was almost concealed. The board proclaiming 'The Thatches' was all but hidden — a bit unusual for a person who wanted to flaunt his existence, she was forced to admit.

She found herself driving through beautifully tended parkland, and was beginning to wonder just how far back from the road the house was set, when suddenly there it was. It was so different from the image she had built up in her mind that she stamped on the brake involuntarily and sat staring at the picture before her.

The house was set long and low, so that it almost seemed to nestle into its surroundings and become a part of them. Dana was impressed, in spite of her determination not to be, and she fell in love with it on the spot.

As she parked her Mini and climbed out, she just had time to notice the roses round the door before a grey-haired woman appeared on the step and urged her to 'Come along in.'

'Mr Mitchell . . . ?' she queried tentatively.

'He's on the telephone at present and can't be disturbed,' she was abruptly informed. 'So if you'll come this way.'

The hallway was wide, darkly panelled, and smelled pleasantly of polish, but Dana barely had time to enjoy it before she was whisked through a doorway on the left, bade to sit down, and left alone.

She was being forced to review each of her preconceived notions one by one, she acknowledged, looking round the comfortably furnished room with rueful pleasure. There was nothing brash about this room; it suited the thatched house admirably, with its chintz-covered chairs and pastel-washed walls, though not the picture she had built up of its owner.

Before she had time to pursue that line of thought further, the woman returned to set down a tea tray in front of her. 'Oh, that's very kind of you,' Dana said gratefully, eyeing the bone-china cup and saucer, and the homemade biscuits.

'You might not get time for tea when you start working,' the woman commented with a deep nod of her tightly permed head. 'I should enjoy it while you can.'

A warning, Dana wondered, watching the plump figure disappear through the door. Refusing to allow the thought to rattle her carefully controlled composure, she settled back in the chair to enjoy her tea and comfortable surroundings while she could.

'Well, you're punctual. That's one virtue in your favour that the others didn't have.'

The deep tones were instantly recognisable and disconcertingly close. Hot tea slopped onto Dana's hand, but she ignored the pain as she rose to her feet and turned in one fluid movement to meet face to face the mean and moody Mr Mitchell. To say that he was not at all what she had expected was, Dana acknowledged dazedly, one enormous understatement. The whole, beautiful room slipped out of focus as she stared at the man standing in the doorway.

Where was the brash, paunchy individual that she had pictured so vividly? Where the balding head and florid features that had become so real to her?

How could he do this to her? It just wasn't fair that she, who had never had so much as a crush on a film star, should feel as if she had been punched in the stomach the very minute she looked into those deep, hypnotic, sea-green eyes.

'Finish your tea,' he urged, adding as he strolled into the room, 'And would those be some of Maggie's wonderful biscuits?'

'Mmm.' The murmur Dana managed was barely audible, and she wondered with barely concealed panic what had happened to the cool and efficient tones that she had been practising so carefully for days.

'Help yourself,' he encouraged her, with a smile that made her toes curl up inside of her shoes, 'or she'll be mortally offended, I assure you. Not one of these women that exist on crumbs, are you?'

The question was totally unexpected, and almost barked at her, as the deep green eyes narrowed to suspicious and disapproving slits that raked her slim figure. The smile had lulled her, momentarily, into a sense of false security, making her forget why she was there, and, more disturbing, the type of man she was dealing with. The question broke the spell and lifted the dangerous lethargy that seemed to have captured her normal no-nonsense attitude.

'Indeed not,' she answered primly, stepping carefully into the role she had prepared for herself.

'I'm glad to hear it.' There was warm approval in the deep, velvet tones, and Dana had to fight not to let it distract her, or let him see how easily he managed to unsettle her.

*   *   *

The phone was ringing as Dana let herself into her front door with a sigh of relief that seemed to come from the depths of her soul. As she lifted the receiver, she acknowledged painfully that the last few hours had been some of the longest and most difficult that she could ever remember.

'How did it go?' Kerry's voice was alive with curiosity, and full of all the energy that Dana enjoyed being around.

'Don't ask,' Dana begged. 'Just don't ask.'

'That bad, huh?'

'On the contrary,' she told the secretary ruefully. 'He was wonderful — couldn't have been more charming. He constantly assured me that I was doing very well, and he seemed most concerned that I was enjoying the work.'

'Isn't that good?' Kerry sounded puzzled. 'He sounds perfect.'

'Mmm. Too perfect,' Dana agreed. 'But he didn't get that reputation of his from nowhere, and those women didn't walk out for no good reason. I feel as if I've been walking on eggshells ever since I got there this morning — and why didn't anyone tell me that he's so good-looking, he makes the blood sizzle in your veins?'

'Is he?'

She sounded so impressed that Dana just had to laugh as she assured her, 'Yes, he is.'

'I see.' Kerry sounded almost peeved. 'Perhaps I should have insisted on going. It sounds as if I'm really missing out.'

'There's got to be more to it.' Dana was almost thinking aloud. 'And I'm almost afraid of finding out what it is.'

'Perhaps you're what he was looking for,' Kerry soothed. 'It was probably that suit of mine. I bet he thought that no one who dressed like that could possibly be anything but efficient. You must have fooled him completely.'

'God help me if he finds out that I'm not what I seem,' Dana said with a wealth of feeling and a deep shudder.

'You'll be fine.'

'I wish I had your confidence, I really do.'

The minute Dana put the phone down, after a little more chatting and many more assurances from Kerry, she rushed to the mirror to stare at her unfamiliar reflection critically. Trying to see with her own eyes what Alexander Mitchell had seen with his was difficult; nigh on impossible, she had to admit. Had she managed to portray the image that she had so desperately strived for? Or did she look the way she felt: like a complete imposter, an incompetent actress, in a role for which she was clearly unsuited? The grey of her eyes was dark and troubled through the tinted lenses of the borrowed spectacles, and she found herself wondering if she was taking the chance of damaging her eyesight along with her reputation. Still, she sighed, they did lend an air of authenticity to her appearance, and Kerry had assured her that they were little more than plain glass.

Dana had never considered herself a beauty, but she had always been at pains to make the best of what she had. Now, taking away the undoubted benefit of cosmetics carefully applied, and with the cloud of her thick dark hair confined in a tight, unbecoming bun, she looked positively frumpy, and the suit was the final touch.

She reached up and began to remove the pins that felt as if they had been skewered permanently into her skull. As her hair was released to fall, dark and thick around her shoulders, the headache she had endured for hours immediately began to lift. With the glasses gone, the depression she felt at her own appearance also began to lighten.

'Okay,' she told her reflection, 'you're not so bad, not really.'

Shrugging out of the baggy suit jacket that had belonged to Kerry in stouter days, Dana went to take a much-needed shower, sliding the loose-fitting skirt down over her slim hips as she went. Under the cascading water she managed to wash away the tension that had seemed to hold her in a vice-like grip for hours, and only then did she allow herself to dwell on the day she had managed to get through with an ease that had surprised and also worried her.

She just could not believe that everything had gone so well. No temper tantrums, no impossible demands; in fact, nothing more difficult had come her way than the typing up of notes and a few letters — all things that any normal secretary could have handled standing on her head. There just had to be more to it, or why had those other women found the job so impossible, and why had Alexander Mitchell found *them* so unsatisfactory?

Dana shrugged, determined that she would just take each day as it came. After all, it wasn't going to be forever — just until Gillian's mother was on the road to recovery, and then her ordeal would be over and she could get back to the sort of normal life that she hadn't known for over two years.

She suddenly realised with a start of surprise that it was the first whole day she had gone through without dwelling at some time, and with great sadness, on the last illness and subsequent death of her father. A whole day when she had had so much on her mind that there had just been no time for the past. She realised that, incongruous as it might seem, the difficult author was helping her to get her life back together. Perhaps, after all, she could be what he needed, because it certainly seemed as if he was just what the doctor ordered for her — though he'd probably be horrified if he knew it. 'Therapeutic' was not a word that would ever have been applied to that man, she felt certain, and the thought made her smile.

When Gillian phoned, Dana was able to assure her with a clear conscience that everything at the agency was under control. She was rewarded by the relief that she could hear so clearly in her friend's voice.

'It's so good of you,' Gillian said gratefully. 'I don't think I could have coped here with the agency to worry about as well.'

'Everything's fine, and every customer is satisfied,' Dana told her. 'Now, how's your mother? Is there any improvement in her condition at all?'

'They're talking about operating, and they say that her chances of a full recovery are very good,' Gillian said, and added almost hesitantly, 'I'd really like to stay . . . '

'Then stay,' Dana urged, 'and don't worry about a thing at this end. Kerry and I can manage.' Her fingers crossed automatically for luck behind her back. 'Stay as long as you need to.'

'Well, if you're sure . . . '

'I'm sure.'

Assuring her friend had seemed to give her own confidence a boost, Dana found, and she fell asleep that night almost as soon as her head touched the pillow, waking refreshed and ready for the day ahead.

Following the chat with her friend the night before and the realisation that she was doing this for Gillian for the best of reasons, dressing in her 'disguise' seemed more of a matter for laughter than regret, and she found herself giggling as she pulled on another baggy blouse and oversized suit, the skirt of which fell to well below her knees. With her hair scraped back once more, and the glasses perched on her small nose, she looked, she had to admit, as if efficiency were far more important to her than appearance.

The drive from her small flat in Bournemouth to the charming house on the outskirts of Salisbury seemed to be accomplished in no time. The lack of heavy traffic on the roads and the September sun glinting on the windscreen all served to boost Dana's new and confident mood of optimism. She was smiling as she reached her destination and climbed from the car.

'Good morning, miss. Lovely day, isn't it?'

'Indeed it is,' she agreed, turning automatically to face the man who had spoken so cheerfully. Watching as he pushed a wheelbarrow full of garden tools towards her, she asked, indicating the grounds, 'Is it your job to keep all this looking so wonderful?'

'That's me. Adam Collins.'

Dana shook the hand he offered, liking his firm grip and pleasant smile. 'Dana Abraham,' she returned.

'Let me guess,' he said, laughing. 'A secretary, are you?'

She found herself grinning. 'However did you know? And — ' She glanced at her watch. ' — I'd better get a move on, or I'll be as short-lived as the rest.'

'Nice to have met you — and good luck.'

With the gardener's wishes ringing in her ears, Dana let herself in at the front door, as she had been instructed to do, and made her way straight to the office.

Alexander Mitchell was there before her. He was standing with his back to the room and staring out of the window as she entered, but he swung round almost immediately and glared at her with such intense dislike that Dana had to fight the urge to back away. Before she had time to wonder what on earth she had done to engender such a look, he snarled savagely, 'I don't pay you to stand around gossiping.'

She looked pointedly at the clock on the wall, which clearly showed that she had fifteen minutes to go before her official starting time, but refrained from actually mentioning the fact. Clearly something had upset him, and she decided that contradicting him could only make matters infinitely worse.

'No, you don't,' she agreed, in what she hoped was an agreeable tone.

'Then perhaps we can get on.' He sounded slightly mollified, and Dana had the feeling that she had either passed a test, or avoided a trap.

'Of course.'

She spent the morning working from recordings that he had apparently dictated while travelling, with instructions to print out the work at the end of the day so that he could make any alterations onto the paper. The computer was very up to date and the programme easy to operate; his diction was easy to follow, and a pleasure to listen to. With a racy storyline, Dana's fingers fairly flew over the keyboard.

'I've put your lunch out in the dining room.' The housekeeper's voice behind Dana made her jump, and she accidentally pressed the delete key, wiping out a line of typing.

'Oh!' She spun round in her chair. 'You needn't have bothered; a sandwich in here would have been fine. Is Mr Mitchell stopping for lunch?'

She suddenly realised that she hadn't seen him for quite some time, and this was explained when the woman said abruptly, 'He had to go out,' and just about managed a stiff smile before turning away.

'Mrs — er, Maggie,' Dana called, adding apologetically, 'I'm afraid I don't know your surname.'

'It's Warrington — Mrs Warrington.'

Dana smiled and asked hesitantly, 'I wonder if I might eat in the kitchen with you. The dining room is a little

42

formal for me, and rather lonely.'

'If you wish.'

The reply was stilted and unfriendly, but at least she hadn't said no. Dana felt as if she had to get this woman on her side, or she would feel very isolated during her time at the house.

She stayed only long enough to eat the delicious homemade soup and the thickly buttered crusty roll before returning to her work, aware that to outstay her welcome would not endear her to the housekeeper at all. Still, she felt she had made a little progress in the right direction and returned, quite happily, to pick up where she had left off.

She was soon immersed in the plot once more, and she jumped again when the author himself suddenly spoke from the doorway. 'Don't you know what time it is?'

Dana looked at him and then at the clock, and was amazed at how late it was.

'Good lord,' she said, 'I didn't realise.'

'You hadn't noticed?' The question was quite friendly; he merely sounded interested.

'I'm afraid I got carried away,' she confessed. 'I'll just print up what I've done so far and be on my way.' She deftly pressed buttons and the printer stirred into life.

'Do you have far to go?'

'Not far. I live in Bournemouth.'

'Well, you get off. I can deal with the rest of this.'

'If you're sure . . . '

'Your family will be worrying.'

It was on the tip of Dana's tongue to tell him that she had no family, but she stopped herself with the reminder that he was not interested in her background and was only being polite. 'Yes,' she agreed, and collecting her bag, she began to move towards the door.

To her surprise he walked with her, opening both the office and the front door courteously, asking her how she was enjoying the work as they went. She was very conscious of the dark-suited figure, tall and handsome, strolling beside her. The faint smell of his cologne tickled her nostrils tantalisingly, and she found she had trouble answering coherently. He seemed not to notice, to her immense relief, but just wished her a good night in that silky voice of his, and then stood watching as she drove away.

What a contrast to the bad-tempered individual of the morning, Dana reflected, wondering if she would actually discover the real Alexander Mitchell while she was working for him. She was conscious that she knew very little about the man, apart from the damning information contained in his file at the office, and she suddenly realised that she wanted to know more.

It was only natural to be curious, she assured herself as she drove along the darkening roads. He was her boss, however temporarily, and there was something, an indefinable something, that fascinated her about someone who was such a complex character.

She ignored the little voice that told her, sensibly, to leave well alone — to just do the job, take the money and run. There was something about Mr Alexander Mitchell that intrigued Dana and, before she left his employment, she intended to find out what made him tick. Just why it was so important for her to know, she had no idea, and she found she was afraid of studying her reasons too closely . . .

3

The remainder of the week passed with surprising speed, the work proving to be neither difficult nor unenjoyable, to Dana's relief. She was, she felt, no nearer at the end of the week than she had been at the beginning to discovering what type of man her boss really was. With him seeming to be on his best and most charming behaviour, it was becoming increasingly difficult for her to believe the dreadful tales that she had heard about him.

Dana did sense, however, that the housekeeper had warmed towards her fractionally, and the woman no longer viewed her presence in the kitchen at meal times with suspicion. The young gardener she only ever saw from a distance, but he never failed to raise his hand in greeting and, as Dana felt she needed all the friends she could make, she was grateful for that.

It was a pleasure to wake on Saturday morning to the realisation that for once she didn't have to don the drab and baggy clothes that had become her uniform and could let her hair fall, straight and thick, to her shoulders. Dressed in jeans and a long sweater, she felt young again, and so carefree that she positively bounced into the office, ready and willing to tackle anything.

'So, what's he really like?'

She was barely through the door before the questions started, and Dana was in a good enough mood not to mind them; she'd have been just as curious in Kerry's place.

'Not the ogre I'd been expecting,' she admitted readily. 'A little tetchy sometimes, it's true, but his reputation is making me more nervous than the man himself is — that, and the fact that I'm terrified he'll find out I'm not what I seem. I can't think now why we started this charade.'

'We made you into what he wanted,' Kerry reminded her, 'so perhaps that's why he seems to have mellowed. You were tailor-made to his very exacting specifications, after all.'

'Mmm.' Dana accepted that Kerry was right, and that if the man hadn't been so hard to please, the deception wouldn't have been necessary. But somehow it didn't make her feel any better. For the first time in her life she was living a lie, and she didn't like it at all. What was more, she felt certain that if Alexander Mitchell ever got wind of the truth, his wrath would be spectacular to see. The very thought sent a cold, unwelcome shiver along the length of her spine, and she began to fervently hope that the duration of the job would be short and uneventful.

Over a well-earned cup of coffee, Dana smiled at Kerry, and congratulated her on the smooth running of the office. 'Gillian will be so pleased,' she said. 'She's lucky to have you.'

'It's nice of you to say so, but my job has been pretty straightforward,' Kerry admitted. 'The office is relatively easy to run, most of the time. You've had the hardest job, keeping Mr Mean-and-Moody happy. He's been the only fly in the ointment, and it would have been understandable enough if you'd decided to just let him go. I know Gillian wouldn't have blamed you. He's been almost more trouble than he's worth.'

'But he sends a lot of custom Gillian's way, doesn't he?'

'Yes.' Kerry screwed up her nose. 'It's strange, when you think about it. He does nothing but complain about the women we send to work for him — and then he recommends the agency to other writers. Funny, that.'

The phone rang then, cutting short the discussion and making the two women look at each other in surprise. The office was never open for business on a Saturday, as the majority of their clients were well aware.

Dana's furrowed brow suddenly cleared. 'It'll be Gillian,' she guessed, watching Kerry pick up the receiver and, sweeping back her red hair, press the instrument to her ear. Her cheerful greeting was cut off halfway and Dana, watching Kerry's eyes widen, stopped in the act of picking up the cups and stared at her curiously.

Kerry snatched up a pad and reached for a pencil, gesturing wildly all the time for Dana to stay where she was and to read the hastily scrawled words. Looking over her shoulder, Dana watched the letters form with growing apprehension.

M and M, she read, *looking for you*.

She gasped as realisation dawned, and mouthed to Kerry, 'Mean-and-Moody?'

Kerry nodded frantically, at the same time saying into the receiver, 'I'll see if I can find out for you.' Placing her hand carefully over the mouthpiece, she told Dana, 'It looks as if he's been trying to reach you. It's about work or something. He's been phoning your flat. He got your number out of the book, apparently. What shall I say?'

There was no time to dither, and Dana suddenly knew with certainty that she wasn't ready to deal with him again

— not just yet. She had looked forward to these two days off, away from the play-acting and tension, and she was going to have them.

'Tell him,' she instructed Kerry, 'that you don't know where I am — that I can't be reached.'

Kerry mimicked biting her nails in mock terror, so that Dana almost burst out laughing, and then she said into the phone, oh-so-politely, 'I'm afraid we have no other number where Miss Abraham can be reached, and the office is officially closed at the weekend. She will, of course, be back to work for you at the normal time on Monday.'

Replacing the receiver with a grimace, Kerry shuddered and told Dana, 'He didn't sound very pleased.'

'Because I'm not at his beck and call out of working hours?' Dana shrugged. 'Even he can't be that unreasonable, surely?'

But for all of her couldn't-care-less bravado in front of the other woman, the call had the effect of spoiling the weekend for her. She felt she had needed time away from the man to recuperate, in readiness for the week ahead. Now he had encroached on that time and, as he had so often lately, managed to creep into her thoughts.

He had no right, she told herself several times over the rest of a weekend spent foolishly hiding in her flat lest he come looking for her, and refusing to answer the phone in case he was the caller. He had no right at all.

* * *

It took a real effort, Dana found on Monday morning, to climb into the loose, unbecoming clothes that were so necessary for the part she had chosen to play. She discovered she resented the fact that she was unable to make the best of her attributes, and she was laying all the blame for her discontent at the feet of Alexander Mitchell.

What was the matter, she asked herself irritably, with a man who couldn't appreciate an attractive woman? Didn't he have the sense to see beneath the surface? Couldn't he appreciate a woman's work without criticising her style of dress and the make-up she wore?

A tight knot of apprehension began to form in her stomach as she slotted her small car into the busy morning traffic, and purely as a means of distracting herself from the day ahead, she began to ponder what might have made him so unreasonable in his dealings with the fairer sex. Someone had let him down, and let him down badly, she decided. It didn't take much to deduce that. Yet he was obviously a very intelligent man, so why would he apply that to the female population as a whole?

She shook her head. Mr Mitchell was a real mystery. Oh well, she thought with a mental shrug, once this assignment was completed and Gillian was back at work, she would never need to see the enigmatic author again. He was, she assured herself, a complication in her life that she could do without.

Parking her car in front of the house, she glanced in the rear-view mirror to check on her appearance, and was horrified to discover that she wasn't wearing the unbecoming spectacles. She had an awful feeling that they were still sitting on her vanity unit at home. With shaking hands she searched through her bag, trying unsuccessfully to reassure herself that they made little difference to the overall impression she was trying to get across. It didn't help, and she was forced to acknowledge that she actually needed the glasses to hide behind when she dealt with Alexander Mitchell. They were her shield, and from behind them she could deal with any hint of sarcasm or unfair criticism without too much of a dent to her confidence. They were part of her disguise — an important part, and she felt that she couldn't possibly face him without them.

From the corner of her eye Dana saw the front door open and, without lifting her head from the task of turning out her handbag, she saw trousered legs approach the car. The search became more frantic, and she was almost physically sick with fear as the certainty became fixed in her mind that after one look into her unadorned eyes, Mr Mitchell would immediately know her for the imposter that she was.

Polished black shoes had come to a halt beside the car before her hands closed around the smooth spectacle case, and she heaved a huge, shuddering sigh of relief. Refusing, yet, to look up, she opened the hinged lid with trembling fingers and placed the glasses very deliberately on her nose just as the door was pulled open.

'I've been trying to reach you, all over the weekend — without success, I might add,' Alexander Mitchell grated irritably. 'Where were you?'

The fear that Dana had endured as he approached the car was swept away on a tide of hot anger that burned through her body and heated her cheeks to bright scarlet. How dare he?

she thought. How bloody dare he? She couldn't remember ever having been so furious. But she felt suddenly strong again, strangely calm, and certainly confident enough to deal with this overgrown, sulky, and demanding schoolboy.

Climbing from the car with studied ease and no sign of hurry, Dana unfolded her length until she stood tall and straight in front of him; then, raising her chin, she looked the author right in the eye before replying, in a singularly indifferent tone, 'I must have been out when you phoned.'

The green eyes narrowed to jade slits and the lips were compressed into a firm, disapproving line, but Dana refused to be intimidated by his show of annoyance. Reaching into the car, she gathered up her bag before slamming the door with unnecessary force.

She turned to walk toward the house, but had barely taken two steps before her arm was seized. 'I asked you a question.' He glared into her face. 'And I'm waiting for an answer.'

'Really?' Dana shrugged his hand off her arm. 'Then I'm afraid you're in for a very long wait.'

'How dare you . . . ' he began.

'No,' she said firmly, 'how dare *you*?'

The shock on his face at being spoken to in such a fashion was almost funny to see, but Dana kept her twitching lips ruthlessly under control, knowing without a doubt that this was not the time to show amusement. This man was singularly lacking when it came to humour if she was any judge of character, and all the charm in the world didn't make up for that.

'You work for me,' he pointed out, 'and that means — '

'Just that,' Dana interrupted. 'That I work for you and my time is yours from nine in the morning until five in the evening from Monday to Friday.' She watched his chin, a stubbornly chiselled square, jut belligerently, and she hurried on before he could get a word in, anxious to say all that was in her head in case her newfound confidence suddenly deserted her. 'Mr Mitchell,' she said, 'you may feel that you own my time during working hours, and I can accept that — it's what you're paying for, after all — but what I can't, and won't, accept is that my free time is also yours.' She took a deep breath, immensely proud of herself. She had managed to keep her tone cool and pleasant, and she had put her point over without once raising her voice.

He stood, tall and silent, and she met his gaze glare for glare. Then, unexpectedly, he began to laugh. She watched, totally mesmerised, as he threw back his dark head and laughed heartily with every appearance of pure enjoyment.

He stopped as suddenly as he had started, but this time there was a definite curve to the well-shaped lips and a twinkle in the green depths of his eyes. 'You're quite right,' he said with a deep nod. 'I deserved to be put in my place. I apologise.'

His apology surprised her almost as much as his sudden laughter had, but she was determined not to show it. 'You're not angry?' she asked, adding hastily, 'Not that you had any right to be, of course.'

'Of course not.' A wry grin pulled at his mouth. 'And, no, I'm not angry. I just sometimes forget that my latest book is not the most important thing in everybody else's life, too.'

What a strange, almost sad, thing to say. It was as if, despite all his material possessions, his life was an empty thing that needed to be peopled by imaginary characters if it was to have any meaning. Dana's anger dissolved as swiftly as it had come. If she wasn't careful, she realised, she would find herself feeling sorry for him. As it was, she found herself saying suddenly, 'I don't mind working overtime some-times, if I have nothing else on. You only have to ask.'

Now, what on earth had prompted her to say that? He'd have her working all the hours God sent, and that was the last thing she wanted. Eight hours a day were quite enough in the company of such an unpredictable man. She began to wonder if she was turning soft in the head.

'I might take you up on that,' he was saying, 'and it's more than I deserve under the circumstances. The way I lit into you the minute you arrived was completely uncalled for. I'm only glad that you had the spirit to stand up to me, instead of dissolving into tears all over my shirt front. I'm afraid I have little patience with tears.'

Well, Dana thought musingly, that little speech explained quite a lot. Unwittingly, by standing up to the man, it seemed as if she might have earned his respect and done herself a big favour into the bargain. She looked up into his face, and immediately wished that she hadn't. It was useless to tell herself that he was just good-looking, because that alone wouldn't have caused her lungs to feel as though they were being deprived of air. Now she knew the reason why she was always so careful to avoid eye contact with him; why she was so familiar, instead, with the square cut of his jaw. It was because, like so many women must have done before her, she was finding it far too easy to succumb to a handsome face and a crooked smile. Spending too much time in his company was going to be a dangerous pastime, and not for all the reasons she had previously supposed.

He smiled and, turning, took her arm and tucked it securely into the crook of his, patting her nerveless hand as he did so. 'Do you know,' he said with surprise evident in his tone, 'I think you and I will deal very well together.' He nodded, adding, 'Very well indeed.'

He led her — like a biddable child, she thought scathingly — not into the office, but straight into Maggie Warrington's kitchen. 'A cup of coffee for Miss Abraham; she's earned it.' He gave a short bark of laughter. 'I think we'd better look after her, Maggie. We don't want to lose this one.' Having said his piece, he marched back out of the room, shaking his head and chuckling as he went.

When Dana finally managed to tear her gaze away from the empty doorway, she found Maggie looking just as bemused as she knew she did herself. She spread her hands out, palms up in a deprecating gesture, and before Maggie could speak, said, 'Don't ask me what, but I must have done something right.'

'That's an understatement,' Maggie insisted. 'I've not seen him like that for many a long day. Well done, lass. Sit down while I pour the coffee, and you can manage a chocolate biscuit, I'm sure.'

It was all too much for Dana. She began to feel quite light-headed, and she could feel hysterical laughter bubbling dangerously near to the edge of her self-control at the thought of first Mr Mitchell and then Maggie becoming all sweetness and light — and all because she had dared to contradict her boss. She sipped the coffee and warned herself sternly not to get used to all the warmth and approval, because only one thing was certain — it couldn't last.

*   *   *

The morning, as far as work was concerned, was wasted for Dana. She found herself constantly daydreaming while listening to the rich timbre of her boss's voice over the earphones instead of the words he was saying. He could have been speaking Dutch for all the sense she was making of his dictation.

She finally began to lose all patience with herself and her own foolishness when she began to see his face on the screen in front of her, and in such clear detail that she finally had to admit that she must have been paying closer attention to the man than she had ever imagined.

It was only natural, she reminded herself, that she should have taken note of the deep green eyes that were a helpful indicator to the sort of mood he was in. She had learned quite early in her dealings with him that they lightened when he was in good humour, and then darkened warningly when he was crossed. When exactly she had taken in the fact that his black hair was inclined to curl, despite the fact that he kept it cut ruthlessly short, she had no real idea.

Dana tried, without success, to dismiss the features that seemed to be imprinted on the screen in front of her, all but obliterating the few words she had managed to type. In the end she gave up the struggle and allowed herself to fill in each detail with infinite care.

There was the warm, smooth tan of his skin, she remembered, and the dark sweep of his brows that were as black as his hair; brows that were raised or lowered expressively, as much an indication of his moods as the depth of colour in his eyes. There was a proud jut to his nose and a firmness to his well-shaped mouth; and between the two were deeply scored lines that made the handsome face appear almost grim when it was in repose. Lines of suffering? Knowing next to nothing about him, it might just be foolish speculation on Dana's part. With a deep sigh, she began to at least try to get some work done.

'How's it going?'

She jumped guiltily, spinning round in her chair as the deep voice spoke to her from the doorway. Her first feeling was one of overwhelming relief that the author couldn't read her thoughts; her second was one of embarrassment that he had caught her with so little work done, and her face flamed guiltily. There was no point in lying, because he could see for himself within a minute exactly how much had been done. There was an aggravating pain starting just behind her eyes — probably caused by tension, she decided — and she pounced on that as an excuse.

'Not so well, I'm afraid,' she said, finding an apologetic tone from somewhere. 'I have a bit of a headache.'

He strode across the room towards her and she tensed immediately, wondering what he intended to do. She almost flinched as he reached across her, and then watched with amazement as he switched of the machine.

'What on earth are you doing?' she demanded, annoyed at his high-handed attitude and fearful that he was going to sack her on the spot for her unprofessional approach to work. A headache was a poor excuse for the lack of work done, and she knew it.

'Looking at that,' he said, indicating the now-blank screen with an impatient sweep of his hand, 'is the worst thing you can do. Leave it for now, and ask Maggie for some pain relief tablets.'

'But,' Dana pointed out, 'there are all these to be done . . . '

'And they'll still be there when your headache has cleared,' he insisted, helping her to her feet so that she stood facing him. Concern showed clearly in the green depths of his eyes. There was no anger there and no trace of impatience, she was pleased to notice, though she was beginning to feel a complete fraud.

She felt obliged to protest, 'I'll be all right. It's nothing.'

'Nothing that was probably caused by my pouncing on you this morning,' he muttered ruefully and, before she knew what he was about to do, he had raised both of his hands, removed her spectacles, and was lightly caressing her temples with cool, firm fingers.

She stared up at him with wide, dazed eyes. Hypnotised by the skilful play of his fingers against her skin, she forgot everything it was so important that she remember. She forgot where she was, the person she was supposed to be, and most important of all, the type of man she was dealing with.

The concern in his eyes was replaced, as he stared down at her, by something else. Something elusive that darkened his irises to the deepest green and took the breath from Dana's throat. She thought he was going to kiss her. She was sure of it, and she was sure that she wanted him to. And then, at the last moment, she came to her senses and jerked back out of his hands and away from the mesmerising touch.

He made no attempt to keep her, but only murmured 'Better?' in that deep, velvet voice of his.

Dana snatched the glasses up and almost rammed them onto her small nose, 'Much,' she stated firmly, 'but I'll get that tablet from Mrs Warrington anyway.'

She marched from the room, dismayed to find that her legs were actually shaking and her cheeks burning. She was actually close to tears by the time she reached the comparative safety of the kitchen.

Maggie Warrington glanced up from the pastry she was rolling and immediately left her task to come over to Dana, asking as she wiped floury hands on her apron, 'What is it, dear? Is something wrong?'

'It's just a headache,' Dana told her, and was horrified to hear a little pathetic sob in her voice. What was wrong with her? She rarely cried, and certainly never over something so ridiculous.

In a matter of minutes, she was ensconced in Maggie's small sitting room, situated to the side of the kitchen, with the lady herself fussing round her and insisting that she must not move until she was completely herself again. It was good to be taken care of, and suddenly Dana missed her father so much that the tears came in a rapid spurt of grief for his passing. She had tried so hard to be strong, but suddenly with the strain of all that had recently happened she found herself wishing for the strength of his arms about her and the knowledge of a love that had never changed. He could have told her what to do, and perhaps he might even have been able to explain why this moody author had been able to get under her skin the way he had.

Why did it have to be him — of all people — who had the power to light fires in a heart that had remained singularly undisturbed through a succession of very nice, normal boyfriends over the years? Why was he so different?

Alexander. She tasted his name on her tongue, and knew with a wry and almost bitter smile why the answer was so easy to find. He was moody, unpredictable and, quite simply, the most exciting man she had ever met or was ever likely to meet.

She should be running away from him as fast as her legs would carry her, if she had any sense. Easy to say — except that she knew without a doubt that good sense had walked out of her life the same day that Alexander Mitchell had walked in.

4

The day didn't improve for Dana, in spite of the fact that her boss was at his most charming and that Maggie had — as though bestowing a royal favour — intimated that Dana may use her Christian name instead of the more formal Mrs Warrington. At the end of it, what had started as almost an imaginary headache had become the real thing, and pain relief tablets had made little impression. She was never so glad to close her own front door, shutting out the problems — if only temporarily.

She found herself snapping at Kerry when she phoned, and then was immediately ashamed of her outburst. She was, she warned herself, getting as touchy and unreasonable as the man she was working for.

'I'm sorry, I shouldn't vent my spleen

on you,' she apologised. 'I have no idea what's the matter with me. I can't even stand myself today.'

'Look,' Kerry said firmly, 'if it's this job that's getting to you, then I really think you should leave. It's just not worth the hassle, and I'm sure that Gillian wouldn't expect so much of you.'

For a long moment, Dana was tempted. Not to have to dress up in ill-fitting clothes, or to play a part; to be able to forget all about typing manuscripts; and most of all, never to have to see that unsettling, unpredictable man, or deal with his moods ever again.

'No,' she finally said, 'I will not let a mere job — ' or *man*, she added silently ' — get the better of me. I can handle it, Kerry. I know I can.'

'We-ell . . . ' The other woman sounded doubtful. 'I suppose you know best.'

'Yes.' Dana's tone was firm. 'I do. Gillian won't lose a client if I can help it.'

Was that the reason she insisted on carrying on? It was a question that Dana found herself asking over and over again during a restless evening spent pacing the narrow confines of her small flat. Of course it was; what other reason could there be?

She didn't really need the money the job paid, generous though it was, since the sale of the house she had shared with her father had brought in enough money for her to buy this flat outright *and* start back up in business again when she was ready. She was doing this solely for Gillian's sake, she reminded herself. To repay her the debt of gratitude that she owed, and for no other reason at all. She nodded her head briskly to dispel any lingering doubts, but then was at a complete loss to explain to herself why, at that precise moment, the image of her temporary boss should suddenly be painted vividly across her mind in meticulous detail, from his highly polished shoes to the top of his springing head of black hair.

The phone rang before she had a chance to explain away the intrusion into her thoughts, and, if she was truthful, she welcomed the interruption. Though she did wonder momentarily who she might discover on the other end of the phone, and if it could possibly be Alexander Mitchell daring to ring her at home after she had told him off so roundly. As soon as it occurred to her, however, she dismissed the idea as foolish and fanciful. Walking briskly across the room, she lifted the receiver, and then was quick to assure herself she was relieved to hear her friend's voice.

'Hello, Gill,' she greeted her friend with warm enthusiasm. 'How's your mother? How are you?'

'She had her operation this morning.' Dana could hear the emotion plainly in the familiar voice. 'And they're really pleased with the way it went, Dana. It's such a relief. We've been assured she has every chance of making a full recovery.'

'Oh, Gillian.' Dana's eyes filled with

sympathetic tears because she knew, only too well, what her friend had been going through. 'I can't tell you how pleased I am. That's wonderful news.'

'I feel so glad that I could be here with her. I'm sure it's made all the difference, and it's thanks to you.'

'Nonsense,' Dana felt bound to protest. 'I've had Kerry's help, don't forget, and she's been an absolute tower of strength. We were both glad to be of help.'

'I've been meaning to ask you,' Gillian went on, 'if you've been having trouble with any of the clients, or perhaps the employees. Whenever I've phoned the office Kerry is very evasive, muttering something each time about you being called out. She sounded so secretive.'

Dana realised she should have been expecting something like this. Gillian was no fool, and it had been a certainty that she would soon start asking questions.

'You can tell me to mind my own business,' Gillian went on, 'because you're doing me a great favour, but I was just concerned that you had some trouble to deal with and didn't want to worry me. I know what you're like.'

Dana couldn't help grinning. She had never been able to keep a secret from her best friend and should really have known better than to try. 'It's nothing, Gill, really. I've just been standing in for one of the ladies, that's all, I promise you. It's not a problem. I'm quite enjoying it,' she lied, crossing her fingers firmly behind her back, and praying that her friend wouldn't ask who the client was.

Gillian laughed lightly. 'Well, as long as you don't mind. In fact, if you change your mind about going back to interior design, I can always use a good, reliable contact on my books.'

They were both laughing as they made their farewells, and only after Dana had replaced the receiver did she realise that she was stiff with tension. She uncrossed her fingers carefully and breathed a huge, heartfelt sigh of relief. There would be time enough for explanations when

Gillian's mother was on the way to recovery and her friend was back in the driving seat at the office again. Then it would be up to Gill what she did about her infamous client, and no longer any of Dana's concern.

She found herself wondering idly as she undressed for bed if Mr Mitchell would miss her at all, and whether he would enquire after her, or maybe even put in a special request that she work for him again. She found herself shaking her head emphatically. No, once Gillian was back and had found him a reliable secretary, Dana was perfectly sure that the man would not give her another thought.

She was quite unprepared for the sharp stab of regret that pierced her usual calm good sense. She knew with a certainty that she was not happy at all at the thought of drifting out of his life without him ever seeing the real person underneath the baggy garments and prim hairdo.

Suddenly she remembered the look

in his eyes that morning when he had been massaging the pain from her temples, and she knew that for a moment he had been as aware of her as she was of him. She remembered, too, the way she had felt when she had thought that he was about to kiss her — and how much she had wanted him to.

Dana's face flamed. She turned to face her mirror, crossing her arms sternly as she glared at her reflection. 'What is it with you?' she demanded of the flushed face staring back at her. 'You've not even known that man two weeks, and you're ready to fall into his arms if he so much as looks at you with a hint of interest. It won't do, my girl. Any man right now would be a complication you could do without — especially *that* man, for heaven's sake.'

She turned away, but not before she had imagined his strong, tanned hands holding her very close. The unlikely image stayed firmly, and annoyingly, imprinted on her mind, and it was a very long time before sleep finally claimed her.

* * *

The drive to work next day gave Dana the chance to lecture herself on the dangers of seeking anything more than a boss/secretary relationship with Alexander Mitchell. As it was, she reminded herself, their whole liaison was built on a lie; she was probably exactly the type of female that he professed to despise.

She glanced distastefully down at yet another overlarge suit that fell well down over what she knew to be shapely enough knees, and she wondered what he would say if she turned up one morning looking as she normally did. Perhaps when Gill was back she would do just that.

For all her worries, surprisingly enough, the rest of the week passed quite uneventfully, with the author on his best behaviour and the work straightforward and enjoyable. By Thursday Dana had relaxed considerably and was able to assure herself that she had her feelings well under control. If things went on accordingly, the work would soon be finished, with herself heart-whole and Gillian's prized client a satisfied man.

She'd seen little of the man himself for most of the day, and indeed for the better part of the week, so she was surprised when he put his head round the door as she switched off the computer prior to leaving for home.

'All set to go?'

It was a harmless enough query, but the accompanying smile almost played a tune on Dana's heart-strings, and she was immediately irritated with herself for allowing him to affect her so easily. The unreasonable annoyance was turned onto the unsuspecting culprit, and caused her to snap waspishly, 'It *is* five-thirty, you know, Mr Mitchell.'

The smile didn't even slip. 'I wasn't criticising, and isn't it about time you called me Alex?'

Oh, that was unfair. Not only was he

smiling at her in a way that would melt the hardest heart and charm his worst enemy, but he was also inviting her to call him by a name that must surely only be used by people who knew him very well. To Dana's recollection, no one phoning to speak to him or leave a message had ever yet called him Alex.

'It wouldn't be business-like,' she protested primly with a disapproving look through the wide lenses of the borrowed spectacles.

He came further into the room and watched as she began to gather up her belongings. He was dressed casually, and Dana tried desperately not to notice the way the denim of his jeans clung to the strongly muscled thighs, and the way his biceps and chest added disturbing contours to what was a very plain black polo shirt.

'I thought we had become friends.' He was watching her closely, and his deliberate scrutiny was making her feel increasingly uncomfortable. 'You don't object when I call you Dana.'

'That's different. You're the boss,' she said stubbornly. Swinging her bag up onto her shoulder, she added, 'Well, I'd better be off — the traffic can be a pain at this time of night and it'll take a while to get home.'

'Why not stay, then, and eat with me?' he offered persuasively, startling her still more. 'The traffic will be lighter later, and Maggie always cooks enough to feed an army.'

'It wouldn't be — '

'Business-like?' he finished for her, adding with a grin, 'I did have something I wanted to discuss with you — about the book. Is that business-like enough for you?'

'You never mentioned anything about this before,' she said suspiciously, fighting a losing battle with her better judgement.

'Did you give me a chance?' he demanded, jutting that square jaw in her direction questioningly. 'You were too busy objecting to calling me by my given name.'

'Your given name is Alexander,' she pointed out weakly, 'according to the front cover of your books.'

'And Maggie's is Margaret,' he reasoned, 'but you don't object to using that. Don't you like my name?'

He sounded so plaintive that Dana felt her resolve weaken. It would be rather nice to think that they could be friends, she began to convince herself, and the thought of one of Maggie's meals set her mouth watering copiously.

'You'll stay?'

'I'll stay.'

'Alex,' he prompted.

With a light laugh, she echoed self-consciously, 'Alex.'

'Wonderful,' he said, looking mightily pleased with himself. 'I'll just go and let Maggie know.'

The minute he had left the room, Dana began to doubt her own sanity. What on earth was she thinking? Dinner *a deux* with Alexander Mitchell was not a good idea at all, nor was it sensible to treat him as a friend. He was her boss, at least temporarily, and it would be far safer for her own peace of mind to keep him in his place, and to stay in hers.

It was too late; he was back in seconds to inform her that Maggie was delighted, and was at that moment laying an extra place at the table. 'I'd offer you a drink,' he said, 'but I know that you'll be driving.' He hesitated fractionally before suggesting, 'You could stay, of course; there's plenty of room.'

'Oh, no, it wouldn't be — '

'I know.' He nodded.

He ushered her into the hall, and then she found herself ensconced in the comfortable sitting room that she had been in on her first day. There was a fire in the grate, and the room was lit by several table lamps that shed a cosy glow onto the chintz furnishings.

Pouring her a mineral water, he commented, 'This is nice. I get very tired of my own company, you know.'

Alone by choice though, surely? was

Dana's immediate thought; aloud she said, 'You could always dine with Maggie.'

He looked suitably horrified, and objected at once. 'I wouldn't even dare to suggest it. I know my place, and it isn't in Maggie's kitchen. You're allowed to spend more time there than I am. I call that quite unfair.'

'Ah, but you're the boss, Mr Mitchell. I am just a worker, like Maggie.'

'Not just a worker,' he interrupted. 'I don't think I've actually told you how very pleased I am with your work.' A sudden frown creased his brow as he added, 'What happened to Alex?'

What, indeed? She was certainly seeing his better side and realised that recently the black moods that seemed to have been his trademark in Gillian's office had all but disappeared; that in fact, except for a couple of minor skirmishes, she seemed to have escaped relatively unscathed during her time working with him. She must have been doing something right.

Then she remembered her appearance, which amounted to a disguise, and her brief pleasure in his compliment died immediately. She doubted if she would have lasted for half a day as her real self, and she was suddenly disappointed in the man who would so hastily prejudge someone by the clothes they wore, giving them no chance to prove themselves.

'I'm pleased if you're pleased,' she said, unable to keep the sudden chill from her tone, and added, almost as an afterthought, 'Alex.'

The green gaze narrowed slightly, and Alex looked as if he were about to say something. He had, in fact, already opened his mouth when Maggie put her head round the door and he closed it again.

'Dinner is served,' she said formally, and withdrew immediately.

Alex offered his arm, for all the world as if this were a real dinner party. Taking it, Dana whispered, 'I feel as if I should be dressed a little differently. I hadn't expected it to be so . . . so . . . '

He grimaced comically and admitted, 'Neither had I.'

They dined elegantly by candlelight, and Dana knew that under different circumstances she'd have been thrilled by the charm and grace, not to mention the good looks, of her companion. He was witty and amusing, and Dana felt she would have had to be a complete idiot not to have enjoyed herself hugely.

The meal was cooked and presented as only Maggie knew how. The soup, piping hot and tasty, was quite obviously homemade, as were the wholemeal rolls that accompanied it. The steak Diane that followed melted creamily onto Dana's appreciative tongue, and though she protested that she could not possibly eat another spoonful, a good portion of the sherry trifle found its way into her stomach.

'Not another mouthful,' she gasped as the trifle spoon hovered again over her dish, 'or I promise you that I shall not be fit for work tomorrow.'

The spoon was dropped immediately back into the serving dish with a gasp of simulated horror, and Alex pleaded, 'Not that — please, not that.'

Dana laughed and pushed away the vague feeling of discontent again that he'd not have been so satisfied with the real Dana. At least Gillian would have reason to be pleased, she reminded herself, knowing that any report he handed in would be a good one. Pointless to wish for the moon, as her father might once have said.

'Coffee?' He smiled, the corners of his mouth lifting and the green of his eyes turning a shade lighter. 'In the sitting room, I think.'

'I must leave soon,' she reminded him gently, 'or it will be time for me to turn around and come straight back.'

'You could always — '

'No.' The answer was emphatic enough, but thankfully Dana knew that he was unaware of the unnerving visions that clouded her brain. Pictures of the two of them meeting at the bathroom door, of them breakfasting together cosily; pictures that were dangerous to her peace of mind, and misleading, to say the least. Pictures that had no chance of becoming reality.

In the sitting room, she sat primly on the edge of a chintz-covered chair — as if poised for flight, she taunted herself bitterly, and she wondered how she had ever managed to feel so relaxed in Alex's company during the meal.

His fingers brushed her hand ever so slightly as he passed her the delicate coffee cup, but it was enough to make her jerk away, slopping the contents generously into the saucer.

'I'm sorry,' he said immediately. 'How clumsy of me. Did it burn you?'

Dana knew it was cowardly, but she had to let him take the blame or he might realise that his touch unnerved her, and that would never do. If he discovered the way she felt . . . She paused, horrified at the turn her thoughts were taking. The way she felt? How did she feel? This was ridiculous.

She felt nothing more for the man than . . . what? She liked him — sometimes. She admired him — sometimes. She was even attracted to him — sometimes. But nothing more; no, nothing more.

'I'm quite all right,' she said firmly, as much to herself as to him, and took the fresh cup that he offered without further mishap, adding, 'You haven't told me what you wanted to see me about.'

He frowned momentarily, and then smiled. 'Ah,' he said. 'A favour. I wanted to ask you a favour.'

'A favour?' She knew she looked doubtful, and made no attempt to hide it. Favours were for friends, she told herself, and she wasn't sure that they were, or ever could be, friends, whatever she had previously thought.

'I have to go away for the weekend,' he began, turning away to pour himself more coffee.

Dana sat very still, as if turned to stone, suddenly sure that he was going to ask her to go with him, but uncertain yet why. She felt her face begin to burn. 'Yes?' she prompted, amazed at her cool tone.

'It's very unfortunate.' He added a heaped spoonful of sugar and stirred it maddeningly and thoroughly before continuing. 'Just when the book is so near to completion, and with a very real hope of meeting the deadline for once, thanks to you. So I was wondering . . . ' He took a sip and turned to look at her suddenly and sharply.

Dana felt as if she were pinned to the chair by his gaze as she waited, her calm exterior hiding a seething mass of emotion. 'Wondering?' she prompted hoarsely.

'If you'd be willing to stay here over the weekend and continue just as you've been doing, in my absence?' When she didn't reply immediately, he rushed on, almost as if he were nervous — which was ridiculous, she told herself. 'I would, of course, pay you well for giving up your leisure time. It'd mean that things don't just grind to a halt; the printed pages would be ready and waiting for me to go through when I get back. What do you say?'

For a long moment she was completely unable to say anything, as she battled with the hysterical laughter that threatened to break the surface of her calm exterior. So he didn't want her to go with him. Had she really believed that he would? Of course she hadn't, she insisted stubbornly; but nor had she been expecting him to invite her to stay in his home for the weekend — with or without him in it.

'I won't be here haranguing you,' he went on. 'You can work entirely at your own pace. I'll be delighted with whatever you achieve, and you won't have the added burden of the long drive back and forth to contend with.'

A tanned hand swept through the dark hair, disturbing the neat style, and Dana was fascinated to see that it settled into the thick black curls that were normally swept away by ruthless brushing. The less severe style made him seem more human, somehow, more boyish in his looks.

Dana shook herself mentally as she realised that while she was mooning over his looks yet again, he was waiting with a great show of patience for her answer. 'Well, I . . . ' she began, and watched his face fall in readiness of the refusal he was obviously sure was coming. 'Yes, all right, I'll do it.'

'You will?'

It was only his obvious and very real pleasure at her sudden acceptance that prevented her from changing her mind immediately, telling him that she had made a mistake and already had other commitments. It was just a weekend of work, she reminded herself irritably; nothing to worry about at all. Her boss wasn't even going to be here. She was every bit as eager as he was to see the book finished and off to the publisher, because only then would she be free to go back to being the person that she really was, free of this deception.

'That's great!' He was boyishly and enthusiastically grateful. 'I felt so sure that you'd say no.'

'I can't think why.'

He grinned. 'I sometimes get the feeling you don't like me all that much,' he admitted, 'and I do accept that I can be difficult to work with sometimes. But I must tell you that I have nothing but admiration for you.'

★ ★ ★

'Nothing but *admiration*!' Dana hurled a hairbrush across her bedroom in an uncharacteristic display of temper. 'But not for *me*. Not the real me. It's for the dowdy Miss Prissy that he thinks I am.'

She glared in disgust at the small suitcase packed with enough of the overlarge outfits to see her safely over the weekend, and then, almost defiantly, she reached into her wardrobe for what was one of her own favourite outfits. Without pausing long enough to allow herself to change her mind, or ask herself why, she put it in the case and closed the lid with a snap.

She'd work, she told herself, long and hard over the weekend. If she had anything to do with it, Alex's precious book would certainly meet his publisher's deadline. He would be pleased, which would be a feather in Gillian's agency's cap, and Dana would be able to get out of the unpredictable author's way, and start to live her life as her own once again.

The thought, she was dismayed to find, did not please her nearly as much as she had expected it would, and she frowned, telling herself that she couldn't — wouldn't — let one man disrupt her life like this. The end result, she was certain, would be only unhappiness, and there had been enough of that in her life already.

5

'I'll show you to your room.'

Maggie pounced on her the minute Dana stepped into the wide hall with her small suitcase held firmly in hand, and a determination to get through the weekend with good grace.

'Thanks, Maggie,' she said, grateful for the warmth of the woman's welcome. 'I hope my staying here isn't putting you to a great deal of trouble.'

'It's no trouble at all.' There was no doubting Maggie's sincerity, and she went on, 'It'll be grand to have another woman in the house for once.'

Dana followed the housekeeper up the broad, carpeted staircase, looking about with undisguised curiosity, and admiring the lovingly polished wood of the curved banister that slid so smoothly beneath the light touch of her fingers.

She made no attempt to hide a gasp

of pure pleasure as Maggie opened a door and ushered her inside. 'Oh, Maggie, this is lovely.' The room was decorated in the lightest of pinks, with a deeper rose in the curtains at the window and mixed into the silver-grey of the deep-pile carpet on the floor.

Maggie smiled. 'I knew you'd like it,' was all she said as she went to open a door on the far side of the room. Waving her hand with a flourish, she added, 'Your bathroom.'

So much for her previous imaginings of meeting Alex at the bathroom door, Dana thought with a wry grimace. Then she reminded herself that he wouldn't be here during her stay anyway, and so there was no chance of them meeting at the breakfast table either. She didn't quite know whether to be pleased or sorry.

'You must work very hard, Maggie,' Dana couldn't help commenting, 'to keep the whole house looking so beautiful.'

'It's a labour of love,' Maggie replied mysteriously, before adding briskly, 'I'll have a cup of coffee waiting for you downstairs.'

Dana hung her borrowed suits up quickly, tucking the unsuitable outfit into the back of the wardrobe hurriedly, with a furtive look over her shoulder. Silly, really, she told herself. No one was likely to come looking through her things, least of all Alexander Mitchell; but it had been an indulgence to bring it at all — and rather pointless, on reflection.

Tucking underwear that was at least her own into drawers that smelt pleasantly of lavender, Dana took one last lingering look around the pretty room that was to be her home for the next couple of days, before making her way downstairs for the promised cup of coffee.

'All settled?'

She was startled to find Alex comfortably ensconced at the big kitchen table with a large sheaf of papers spread out in front of him. His suit jacket was hung from the back of his chair, and he had pushed the sleeves of his white silk shirt up almost to his elbows.

'Quite comfortable, thank you,' she said primly, feeling obliged to take the seat next to him as Maggie set her cup down there.

'Now,' he said, becoming quite brisk, 'everything is set out in some kind of order on your desk, and I'm sure you know what you're doing by now without me going into endless detail. Do what you can with it all, but I don't expect you to spend your entire weekend working.' He paused and looked at her sternly, the green eyes glinting. 'And I shall be annoyed if you do.'

'Yes, sir.' Her lips twitched.

He poked his head forward and, looking right into her eyes, he asked suspiciously, 'Are you laughing at me, Dana?'

His face was so close to hers that their noses were almost touching, and suddenly Dana had never felt less like laughing. There were tiny gold flecks in the deep green of his irises, and she found herself staring at them in fascinated wonder. She could smell the faint tang of cologne on the smooth skin, and she held her breath to savour the scent, as if to hold it safe in her memory forever.

'No,' she whispered, and forced herself to drop her gaze, tearing it away from the hypnotic hold of his and searching desperately for something — anything — normal to say.

'More coffee, anyone?'

Thank heavens for Maggie. Her timely interruption normalised the charged atmosphere, and Dana could have kissed her. 'None for me, thanks,' she managed in a relatively normal tone of voice. 'I must get on with some work or Mr . . . Alex,' she corrected clumsily, 'will think that he's paying me too much.'

'Whatever it is, it's not enough,' she heard him say, but she refused to be drawn and continued her progress through the kitchen door on legs that were not quite steady.

'Just let him hurry up and go,' she murmured, almost falling into her chair. 'I'll work day and night if it'll get me out of here any quicker.'

She heard an aggravating little voice inside her head taunting her with the words *liar, liar* over and over again, but she dismissed it and threw herself into the work that waited with as much enthusiasm as she could muster.

Unfortunately, Alex didn't seem to be as keen to leave as Dana was to see him go. In fact, he seemed to spend the entire day either leaning over her shoulder to see what was on the screen, or apologising for interrupting because there was some point he wished to discuss before he went. She began to wonder how he had ever written a book before in his life without her help if it was really so necessary to ask her opinion on this or that at every turn. By the end of her normal working hours, Dana's nerves were at screaming point, and Alex still showed no sign of leaving. The familiar hands were planted once more on either side of her keyboard, and she could feel his warm breath stirring the tendrils of hair that had escaped the confines of the normally neat little bun.

'It's five thirty,' Alex said unnecessarily, and she gritted her teeth and resisted — just — the urge to tell him to go away.

'I know,' she said, also resisting the urge to run a light hand along the tanned forearm that was so tantalisingly close to her cheek. She supposed she should be grateful for the small mercy that he was totally unaware of the effect he had on her, and could imagine his horror if he imagined for one minute that she had designs on him.

'Shouldn't you be thinking about finishing for the day?' he said.

'Shouldn't you be thinking about leaving, if you're to get to London in time for your meeting?' she countered, striving to keep the irritation from her calm tone.

'Bossy, aren't you?' She could hear

the smile in his voice, and could only wish heartily that he would go back to being the arrogant bully who had been so easy to dislike. It had made life much less complicated. Every nerve ending in her body seemed to be screaming at his close proximity. Didn't he feel the charge, almost like an electric current running between them?

Dana stirred restlessly, and the movement brought him upright and away from her. She immediately and contrarily wanted him back close again, and began to wonder if she were going quite mad.

'I suppose I had better get off.' It sounded suspiciously as if he were reluctant to leave.

'Yes.'

'I doubt if I'll be back much before Sunday evening, as I have one or two other things to see to in town. You'll still be here?'

She nodded. 'I did say I would stay till Monday.'

He smiled again. 'Yes, you did, didn't

you, Dana? And I expect you always keep your promises.'

He sounded as if he were quite confident of her answer, and she'd have liked to answer contrarily, 'Not always' — but it would have been a lie, because she did always try to keep a promise. Like the one she had made to Gillian to look after her business — the one that had got her into this mess in the first place.

'Yes, I try.'

He laughed loudly, as if her answer made him happy, and striding back to her he almost lifted her from the chair. 'Where did she find you, Dana, this boss of yours? You're what I've been looking for, for most of my life — and suddenly, here you are.'

His kiss was sudden, exuberant, and totally unexpected. His lips owned hers, moulding them to his own, and caressing them with an expertise that overwhelmed her. Heat licked along her veins with tongues of flame — and that, too, was sudden, leaving desire and fierce longing in its wake.

He released her slowly, and the shock that she felt was mirrored in the deep, dark green of his eyes. Hot colour burned along his jawline, and somehow he looked — Dana searched dazedly for the word — *uncertain* of what he had started.

He trailed a light finger along the deep blush of her cheek and whispered in a tone that sent her pulse racing out of control, 'Wait for me.' And then he was gone.

Dana heard him take his leave of Maggie; heard the front door slam and his car start up and drive away; and still she stood as though rooted to the spot. She raised shaking fingers to touch the lips that still tingled from his kiss — a kiss that seemed to have seared her very soul and branded her his forever. She tried — she really did try — to tell herself that it was only a kiss, but she came nowhere near to fooling herself. What it had meant to Alex, she had no idea; only that he had seemed as shocked as she had been herself. What it had meant to her, she was barely able to explain.

Could a single kiss change your whole life? She would have said an emphatic no — until now. Could a single kiss make you fall headlong and single-mindedly in love with a man you barely even knew? She would have said a resounding no to that, too — until now.

'Alex.' His name sighed past the lips that he had owned for what had seemed like long heart-stopping minutes, but had probably in reality been only seconds.

Wait for me, he had said. Just that, nothing more — no promises or declarations, just a request to wait. But, for now, it was enough.

⋆ ⋆ ⋆

The evening passed in a blur. Dana ate with Maggie, and she knew that they must have talked but had no idea what about, or indeed, what she had eaten. She worked for a while just to hear Alex's voice, typing mechanically and savouring the deep tone that sounded like music to her sensitive ears.

Her dreams, when she retired to bed, were filled with scenes of Alex declaring his love for her and telling her that he couldn't live without her. By morning she was dreaming of the wedding.

Reality only began to intrude when, in the cold light of day, Dana reached into the wardrobe for the outfit she would wear. She stared at the unflattering navy suit in dawning horror, and all her carefully erected dreams tumbled down around her ears. *Wait for me* . . . The words mocked her now, because she was at last forced to acknowledge that the person Alex had asked to wait for him didn't even exist. He didn't know the real Dana — and when he did, he would see that she wasn't what he was looking for at all, but all that he disliked most in a woman.

Perhaps he need never know, never see the real person. Her desperate heart lurched with a sudden surge of hope — and then it faded and died almost immediately. She had fallen for him, head over heels; she knew that now. Loved everything about him — even the mood changes that were so much a part of who he was — and probably had from the very start. Dana knew that loving him that way meant, for her, honesty and truth, not lies and deceit.

She would tell him, she decided as she trailed slowly down the stairs. Perhaps he would understand. It was a vain hope, and she knew it, but it was all she had.

'You look pale, dear. Did you sleep badly?'

Maggie's concern was touching, but it was nearly Dana's undoing, and she was dismayed to feel hot tears pricking at the back of her eyelids. She blinked rapidly and managed a wan smile. 'I expect it was being in a strange bed,' she replied, because it seemed easier to do so. Her tone was level and quite normal, she was relieved to note, showing none of the turmoil that raged inside of her.

'Well, have a good breakfast and don't work too long today,' Maggie advised kindly, placing a full plate in front of her.

'I'll never eat all that!' Dana found a smile from somewhere in her effort not to upset the housekeeper.

'I'm just following Alex's instructions.' Maggie was completely unperturbed. 'He especially said that I was to look after you, and that's what I'm doing. You just eat as much as you can.'

'I'll do my best. It looks delicious.'

Dana picked up her knife and fork and found to her surprise that she was hungry. Maggie made a fresh pot of tea and settled herself comfortably at the other end of the table.

'Have you worked for Al — um, Mr Mitchell very long, Maggie? He seems very fond of you.' The question wasn't asked idly, though Dana tried to make it seem as though it was. She was beginning to realise that she knew very little indeed about the man she had fallen so swiftly, desperately, and inadvisably in love with.

'Oh, I call him Alex, too,' Maggie told her proudly. 'He's almost like a son to me, and he's always insisted on it.' Her pale blue eyes were suddenly dreamy as she repeated, 'Like a son, and he certainly needed a mother when I first came here.'

Maggie was talking almost to herself, and Dana held her breath so as not to disturb her flow of thought.

'My husband was gardener here before young Alex was ever born.' Maggie nodded, as if remembering. 'I was brought in to take care of the boy the day after his mother left, and I was still here years later to take care of him when his wife left him in the same way, and for the same reason.'

Dana was stunned. Alex had been married? He had never said — but then, it was hardly the sort of thing you told your secretary, she supposed. Why had she left? Were they divorced? Did he still love her?

'She was a very beautiful woman, as lovely as his mother had been.' Maggie sighed gustily. 'You'd think he would know better, wouldn't you, than to repeat his father's mistake?'

'What mistake was that, Maggie?' Dana dared to ask.

The woman looked at her in surprise, as if the answer was something that she should already know. 'Why, to marry someone only interested in the bright lights. That sort would never be happy tucked away down here, but neither of them could see it.'

There was silence for a long moment, and Dana, watching her food congealing on the plate, found that her appetite had quite deserted her. Maggie poured more tea for both of them and they drank, each of them lost in thought.

'He seems very taken with you.' Maggie was the first to speak, and there was warm approval in her voice.

'I don't know why he should be. I'm

only here doing the job I'm paid for.'

'You're a nice, sensible girl with no airs and graces.' Each word from the older woman's lips was like a well-aimed pin, piercing the bright bubble of Dana's hopes and dreams. 'The others were too much a reminder of the women who had let him down so badly.'

'Surely,' Dana had to say, 'Alex knows that all women, even those who like fashionable clothes and make-up, aren't necessarily carbon copies of the two women in his life who let him down? He should surely realise that just because a woman takes a pride in her appearance, it doesn't always follow that she'll find it impossible to settle down.'

'I doubt if he's prepared to take that chance again. I expect you've seen him in the gossip columns with some very lovely women on his arm?' Maggie looked at her expectantly, and Dana didn't feel it was the time to admit that she had never seen the man before she arrived on his doorstep. 'He's never,

ever brought any of them home. It seemed to make him uncomfortable even having those pretty secretaries working here — until you came.'

It was meant as a compliment, Dana knew, but it caused her to sit at the computer feeling more depressed and unhappy than she'd felt since the day her father had died. She found herself bitterly regretting her hasty decision to take on the job as Alex's secretary.

Why didn't I leave well enough alone? Dana mourned. *I could have been happy enough with my career restarted, and my life on an even keel once again.* She found herself seriously doubting that, after the heady delight of Alex's kiss and the temptation of those tantalising dreams, she could ever attempt to go back to her previous existence. If only she'd been honest from the start — and if only she had really been the woman that Alex wanted.

The day crawled slowly on and, somehow, neat pages of manuscript were typed and printed, though Dana's mind was everywhere but on the work she was doing. By mid-afternoon her nerves were jangling with the indecision of how to greet Alex on his return. Part of her wanted to face him, make-up in place, and admit right away to the act she had put on — for his own benefit, as she would soon point out. Another part of her wanted to go slowly, to see first what he had to say — if anything — and go on from there. Yet another part, the coward in her, wanted to leave everything as it was and pray that he would still be interested when he did — as he surely would — discover her deception.

'Come away from that machine and have a nice cup of tea,' Maggie poked her head round the door to urge. 'You've barely left the thing all day. It can't be good for your eyes. No wonder you have to wear glasses. And I've just taken a batch of scones from the oven,' she added, as if that clinched the matter. It probably did, as far as she was concerned.

'Thanks, Maggie.' Dana set the

printer into action and rose stiffly from the chair. 'I'll be right there.'

She heard the deep rumble of a male voice and paused outside the kitchen door, longing for it to be Alex and, at the same time, terrified that it actually might be. Her hand trembled as she reached for the handle and slowly pushed the door open.

'Hello.'

There was no mistaking, now, the cheerful tones of the gardener — Adam, she remembered — to whom she had chatted so briefly in her first week of working for Alex. He was smiling that open, friendly smile that saved his face from being ordinary and made you want to smile back. She did just that.

'Hello.' Dana had no qualms about taking the seat next to him. 'Are you working this weekend, too?'

'Getting ready for winter. You know, bulbs and so on.' He lifted a plate of scones and held them tantalisingly under her nose. 'Not on a diet, are you?'

'Not much point when Maggie's around,'

Dana said ruefully as she helped herself to one and buttered it liberally.

It was cosy in the warm kitchen, the chat round the table was general and, for the first time all day, Dana felt herself relaxing. The tight knot of tension at the base of her skull began to unravel slowly, and she even managed to laugh once or twice.

Maggie was chatting about her family, the sister who lived close by in the village, the brother who lived in Salisbury itself. 'We usually get together of a Saturday evening,' she explained, 'but I shall give it a miss this time.'

'Oh, why's that?' Dana asked idly, thinking that perhaps she disliked going out now that it was darker in the evening.

'I couldn't go and leave you here alone.' Maggie looked most put out at the thought. 'It wouldn't be right.'

'But you must go!' Dana felt dreadful to think her being there was instrumental in stopping an outing that Maggie obviously looked forward to from week to week. 'I won't hear of you cancelling your visit because of me.'

'What will you find to do?' Maggie asked worriedly, obviously torn between pleasure and duty. 'I won't have you spend the evening working. No, I think I'd better stay here.'

'I'll look after her,' Adam offered, adding as they both turned to stare at him, 'All above-board. I've got a girlfriend, but she's away at college. A crowd of us usually meet in the Plough in the village. I'll even pick you up if you fancy a drink.'

'Oh, yes!' Maggie looked delighted at such an easy solution to her problem. 'Do go. It will do you good to get out and mix with people your own age — a real tonic.'

Dana didn't hesitate; the offer was much too tempting. It was a chance to forget, if only for a little while, the problem she had been wrestling with all day. The alternative didn't really bear thinking about — an evening spent in a silent house, longing for and dreading Alex's return the following day, and what that might mean.

'I'll come,' she said, adding only, 'You're sure that I won't be in the way?'

★　★　★

The house was silent as Dana showered; Maggie had left the minute the evening meal was cleared away. Looking unfamiliar in a smart black dress and high-heeled shoes, she'd refused Dana's offer of a lift, explaining that her sister would collect her on her way through.

Dana envied Maggie the chance she had to fold away the pinafore that was almost a uniform and dress up for once. She lifted a black suit from the wardrobe and eyed it distastefully — ugly, ill-fitting thing that it was. Almost in slow motion and of its own volition, her hand replaced the drab garment and moved steadily along the rail until she found what she was looking for.

Tonight, she told herself firmly, *you are going to be Dana Abraham — the real one.*

6

Dana was having the time of her life. For the first time since Alexander Mitchell had made his first appearance on her horizon, she was actually being herself again and enjoying every minute, against all of her expectations.

Adam had insisted on picking her up at the door, saying that Maggie had told him how hard she'd been working, and that it seemed to him that it was time she had a little rest and recreation. 'Just let me know the minute you feel you've had enough of the gang,' he said, 'and I'll bring you straight home. No messing.'

He was a nice, uncomplicated guy, she decided, but his obvious devotion to the pretty blonde girl whose photo he'd displayed so willingly earlier in the evening hadn't stopped his eyes from widening appreciatively when Dana had opened the front door to him. 'Wow,' he'd said.

She'd laughed, pleased by his typically male reaction in spite of herself. She did wonder briefly if it would have been Alex's reaction too, and had to admit that it probably would not — and then she decided not to let any thought of him ruin what promised to be an amusing evening.

Tonight Dana had let her hair down, literally, and it fell in a thick, glossy mass past her shoulders. Her face was skilfully but lightly made up, with the emphasis on the wide grey eyes that she privately thought were her best feature. The outfit that she had packed, against her better judgement at the time, was another suit, but there any similarity to the baggy clothing she had recently been wearing ended. This suit was a smart navy affair, made of a silky material. The jacket was fashioned in a long-line figure-hugging style that effortlessly skimmed her narrow waist, while the skirt was short and pencil-slim. Beneath the suit

Dana wore a lace camisole of the same navy shade, lined with flesh-coloured material, so that it looked more daring than it actually was.

The shoes she wore were slightly lower than she would have liked, but her favourite spindly stilettos were one thing that she hadn't thought to pack. Still, all in all, she was pretty pleased with her appearance. Her one doubt, that she might feel overdressed, was dispelled the minute she was ushered into the lounge bar of the Plough by Adam, and introduced to a crowd of young people who wouldn't have been out of place in the most fashionable up-market bar in London itself.

She was welcomed with a warmth that both surprised and pleased her, and was soon part of the laughing and slightly noisy gang. For the first time in a very long time, Dana felt no older than her twenty-six years; and indeed, by the time the evening was drawing to a close, she was actually feeling very much younger.

The wine had played its part, of course — she knew that; and by the third glass, the last knot of tension seemed to dissolve and she had managed to forget that she had anything at all to worry about. She was grateful to Adam for having volunteered to stick to soft drinks, allowing her the chance to unwind.

'Are you having a good time?' He seemed genuinely concerned that she was enjoying herself, and when she nodded happily, he added, 'I'm glad,' and slipping a friendly arm around her slim shoulders, he gave her a quick hug.

'Put her down, Adam,' one of the guys called from the bar. Dana, laughing, looked across the room for the man who had spoken — and instead, found herself staring right into a pair of unmistakable deep green eyes.

The laughter died on lips that were suddenly stiff, and she looked quickly away, telling herself that surely he wouldn't dream that she was the woman he expected to find at home — waiting. Dressed as she was, and made up, too, he would surely never recognise her. She would be quite safe from discovery as long as she kept her cool.

A deep breath calmed her just a little, but it couldn't slow the rapid beat of her heart or answer the questions that ran through her mind with such speed that they made her feel dizzy. Why was he back? He wasn't due until tomorrow night. And why was he here? Not looking for her, surely? It was the last place he'd expect to find his prim secretary.

Dana made very sure that she didn't turn round again. Let him try to identify her from the back of her head if he could, she told herself. A head with a flowing mane of hair instead of the prim hairstyle that he was used to would surely put him off the scent, if the rest of her appearance didn't.

No, he hadn't recognised her. She became more certain as the minutes passed without him marching across the pub to demand what she was doing there, and she breathed a heartfelt sigh of relief.

'Isn't that your boss over there?' someone asked, and Adam after a quick look raised his arm in casual greeting.

'Wonder what he's doing here?' he mused. 'Not one of his usual haunts.' He gave Dana a straight look. 'He won't mind you being here, will he?'

'Good lord, no,' she denied with far more conviction than she was feeling. 'Why on earth should he?'

'No reason that I can think of.' Adam shrugged and dismissed the subject with an ease that Dana envied.

She longed to ask, when several long minutes had passed, if Alex had left yet, but she was quite sure that he hadn't, and she felt as if those searching green eyes were boring holes in the back of her skull.

She was angry suddenly. How could he do this to her? In seconds he had ruined her composure and all her enjoyment of the evening. He even made her ashamed of her own appearance, and surely that couldn't be right, could it? She felt a strong urge to march up to where he stood and simply tell him to buzz off, but when she looked round at last he was gone, and she didn't know whether to be glad or sorry.

It was none of his business what she did with her spare time, Dana reminded herself hardily. She had actually told him as much only a few short days ago — and he had agreed with her. The thought helped a little, but somehow it didn't help when she tried to tell herself that it was none of his business, either, when it came to her appearance. She had deliberately misled him, there were no two ways about it, and the girl he had kissed was not the real Dana at all. She had a strong feeling that Alex was going to be very, very angry, and she didn't know how she would be able to deal with that, or what she could say in her own defence.

Her troubled thoughts were interrupted by the landlord calling last orders, and a chorus of groans from the customers.

Dana looked up with a start to find Adam watching her, and she immediately pinned a bright and very false smile on her face.

'Shall we go now?' he offered. 'Beat the rush.'

She found a light laugh from somewhere, but couldn't dispel a deep-rooted feeling that he was reading her mind, and very accurately at that.

'Yes, I'd like to get back.' Dana fiddled with her bag nervously, and was annoyed to find herself wishing that she had never come. 'Thank you for bringing me. I've had a great time.'

'He doesn't own you, you know,' he reminded her quietly as they drove away from the pub, as if sensing her disquiet. 'I know he can be a bit unpredictable, but he can hardly grudge you a couple of hours off.'

If only that was all there was to it, Dana thought sadly to herself. Aloud, by way of explanation, she said, 'It's just that I've had such a good time, and I really don't feel like a confrontation tonight. If there's going to be one, I'm sure I would be better equipped to deal with it after a good night's sleep.

'Understandable,' Adam said with a nod, offering no other comment, and Dana thought again what a very nice, uncomplicated person he was.

'If we drive on for a bit,' he was saying helpfully, 'there's another way in, a gate that leads into the kitchen garden. You could go in that way, and no one would see you. Have you got a key to get in?'

She nodded and murmured, 'You must think me very silly.'

'Not me,' he denied at once. 'Anything for a quiet life, that's me — as my girlfriend would tell you. And luckily, she feels the same.'

Adam brought the car smoothly to a halt beside a large wooden gate, getting out to open first the car door and then the heavy gate for her, offering, 'I could walk to the house with you. It's a bit dark in there.'

'I'll be all right.' Dana peered in front

of her. 'I can see the house from here, and the path is quite clear. Thanks again, Adam, for everything.'

'Anytime.' He gave a brisk salute. 'It was a real pleasure.'

Dana crept towards the dark building like a thief in the night, relieved to see that not one light was showing. She assured herself with hearty bravado as she drew closer that Alex and Maggie would be both tucked up in bed and completely unconcerned about her own whereabouts.

The key slid smoothly into the lock, despite fingers that trembled, betraying her nerves, and turned with equal ease. Dana stepped forward into the thick blackness of the hall with a deep, heartfelt sigh of relief and, slipping her shoes off, she tiptoed silently towards the stairs.

'Cinderella, I presume.'

Dana gave a muffled shriek, and at the same moment the hall was suddenly bathed in a brilliant light that pinned her, momentarily blinded, to the spot like a startled rabbit.

Alex — tall, dark, and forbidding — leaned with deceptive ease against the carved banister post. Dana could almost feel the heat of his anger radiating towards her, and she had to force herself not to turn and run out into the safe haven of the night.

'So.' It was almost a sigh. 'It *was* you.'

Dana squared her shoulders and simply said, 'As you see.'

He nodded, his face grim, the lines from nose to mouth deeply etched. 'Why did you do it?'

She deliberately misunderstood him. 'I just felt like an evening out.'

'With the *gardener*?' It was said with a sneer, and Dana felt her own temper rising to her rescue at last.

'Do you have a problem,' she asked icily, 'with two members of your staff going out together? I wasn't aware that there were rules to govern such matters.'

She watched, fascinated, as hot colour swept along the rigid jawline and his fists clenched until the knuckles were white. She felt as if she were playing with fire — a fire that would soon be raging out of control.

'I can do without the pair of you making sheep's eyes at one another on my time,' Alex ground out.

'What reason can you possibly have for making an assumption like that?' Dana demanded angrily. 'We went for a harmless drink with some of his friends. That's all there was to it.'

She was about to add that Adam already had a very nice, steady girl-friend, when Alex interrupted her to mimic with unerring accuracy, 'Thanks again, Adam, for everything.' 'Anytime. It was a real pleasure.'

For a moment she was too stunned to speak, and she felt her face burn with mortification at the implication he had so obviously put on those innocent words, and by the very fact that he had been spying on her. 'You were listen-ing!' She could hardly believe that he would stoop so low. 'How dare you?'

'I was walking,' he stated with no apology, 'in my own garden.'

'In your *vegetable* garden?' She made no effort to hide the disbelief that was clear in her disgusted tone. 'In the pitch dark?'

'I don't believe that I have to ask your permission,' he ground out, 'to walk wherever I will in my own garden, at whatever time I choose.'

'And I,' she interrupted furiously, 'don't have to ask your permission to go out in my own time and with whomever I choose. I'm your employee, not your prisoner. I only worked this weekend to help you out — and I wish now that I hadn't bothered.'

Dana grasped her flagging courage in both hands and marched across the vast hall to pass Alex with her head held high. She had her foot on the first stair and was staring freedom in the face, when Alex's hand snaked out to grasp her arm in that vice-like grip she had suffered once before.

'Not so fast.'

In her elevated position, her face was, for once, on a level with his, and she glared at him, matching stare for cold stare before she hissed, 'Just take your hands off me. Who do you think you are?'

'I'm your boss,' he replied evenly. 'The one who hired you at face value, and now I demand an explanation. Just who are you, Dana, and what exactly is your game?'

She quailed in the face of his anger. It was hard to think rationally when the heat of his fingers burned through the silk sleeve of the offending suit, and the deep hypnotic green of his eyes held her motionless. She couldn't help noticing, though she hated herself for doing so, how smooth and tanned the skin of his face was, and how full and tempting was the firm line of his mouth.

She licked her own lips nervously, closing her eyes for a brief moment before she said huskily, 'It's late, Alex. Surely this can wait until the morning?'

Her own pleading tone annoyed her beyond bearing, and she felt obliged to remind him, 'I seemed to be what you wanted when you gave me the job.'

He gave a harsh laugh and hauled her closer yet as he growled, 'Oh, you were what I wanted.' She watched, mesmerised, as the green gaze raking her face darkened with unmistakable desire, and she shivered as he added softly, 'Unfortunately for me, you still are.'

Her eyes had already closed when his lips claimed her own. The outside world, and the problems that had threatened to engulf her only moments before, were all forgotten in the raging torrent of need that swept through her veins like molten lava.

At first he was angry. It was there in the lips that possessed her mouth, and in the arms that held her to him like bands of steel. Just when it changed, Dana couldn't have said, but almost imperceptibly his lips gentled until they were coaxing her own to part, allowing him to taste the sweetness of her mouth, their tongues to meet and melt.

If he hadn't been holding her she would have fallen, she knew. Closer he held her, and closer yet, and she knew, without a shadow of a doubt, that in his arms was where she wanted to be for the rest of her life. Silly, impossible; but when he held her like that she began to dare to hope . . .

Her heart cried out silently with longing, and she answered his kiss with all the passion that had been missing from her life until now. He wanted her. In spite of everything, he still wanted her. And for now, it was all that mattered.

★　★　★

In the morning, when she faced him with the desk standing like an insurmountable barrier between them, it was as if that kiss had never been. The tender look that had been so clear in his eyes when he had reluctantly released her the night before had been replaced by one so full of cynicism that to Dana it felt like a slap in the face.

She had dressed, after a great deal of heart-searching, not in the overlarge outfits that had become her uniform, but in the silk skirt of the navy-blue suit and with one of the outsize blouses belted neatly over the top. She was very aware that it emphasised the narrow span of her waist and the fullness of her breasts, but she felt it was pointless now to hide what Alex was already familiar with. His hands had circled that waist, and her whole body had crushed close against his own as he held her in his arms.

She now realised that she might just as well have been dressed in sack-cloth and ashes, because Alex was showing her, all too clearly, that the way she looked was of no interest to him except for what it meant in terms of her deceit.

'Alex . . . ' Her hand was stretched out in supplication towards him, and there was a plea in her voice. A plea for understanding, and for him to remember what had been and what might yet be between them.

He ignored the hand and he dismissed the plea, keeping his gaze steadily on her face. The green of his eyes was flat, hard, and disapproving. Then, slowly and insolently, he allowed his gaze to rake her slim body from the top of her shining fall of hair to the tips of her shiny patent shoes.

'Perhaps you would be good enough to explain,' he said heavily, in a voice dripping with sarcasm, 'why baggy, unbecoming suits were the order of the day for me, along with glasses that were patently not needed, and a hairstyle favoured by women twice your age? And,' he went on, as if he guessed that she was about to interrupt, 'why young Adam Collins was treated to the version of a Dana that could have graced the best soap opera without looking out of place?'

It could have been a compliment, but spoken in that tone it would never have been mistaken for one. He was still very angry, Dana realised, and she knew that it was going to take her all her time to try and convince him that it had, after all, only been a harmless deception that had really hurt no one.

'I guess,' he went on relentlessly, 'that the Miss Prim and Proper look wouldn't have impressed a young red-blooded male like Collins, and should only be reserved for an old stick like me.'

That comment was unfair in the extreme, and it quite took Dana's breath away, especially as Alex couldn't have been more than a handful of years older than Adam, who was in his late twenties.

'That's not true, and not fair,' she protested.

'Are you telling me,' he said, his voice as smooth as silk, 'that you didn't get dressed up to the nines especially to show off your many charms to my gardener?'

'Oh — you . . . ' Words failed her for a moment, and she was still — in spite of everything — too controlled to use the name for him that sprang so easily to her lips.

'Yes?' he drawled hatefully, as if willing her to go on and damn herself forever in his eyes.

'It was,' she bit out finally, 'an innocent evening out with a friendly crowd, an invitation probably offered on the spur of the moment, and you're trying to make me feel like a — a — jezebel for accepting.'

'Oh yes,' he said with a nod, adding with a distasteful curl to his lip, 'I saw just how friendly it was. The guy was all over you.'

It was too much, and Dana's rigid control finally snapped. 'You — ' She stabbed a forefinger across the desk at him, wishing heartily that it were something more substantial. ' — have said quite enough. I don't have to stand here and listen to you invent something that never happened. You, Mr Mean-and-Moody Mitchell, have a grubby mind. I wouldn't let Adam's girlfriend hear what you just said, because if you upset her you'll have Adam to deal with, and you might just get the black

139

eye that you so richly deserve.'

She was halfway to the door before
the sound of hearty laughter stopped
her in her tracks and she spun round to
say fiercely, 'Along with all your other
dubious attributes, you obviously have a
very warped sense of humour. Well, I'm
glad you find it funny, because I find it
all rather distasteful, to say the least.'

Dana's hand was on the door handle;
all that was on her mind was getting out
of this obnoxious man's house at the
earliest opportunity. She wanted to be a
part of the sane world again, living a life
that bore no resemblance to the emo-
tional roller-coaster that she had been
experiencing of late. The handle had
turned and the door was opening before
Alex's deep tone stopped her again, try
as she might to ignore it.

'Don't go.'

Two little words, so short, so simple,
that it should have been easy to ignore
them. Was he asking her to stay? Was he
telling her? Was he daring her to defy
him?

Her feet, Dana found, refused to move forward — but she refused to turn back. In the end, she stood, unmoving, and feeling extremely foolish, in the doorway.

'There's nothing more to say, is there?'

'There's everything to say.' He was standing, suddenly, right behind her. She was furious with herself for being so conscious of his nearness that her nerve endings fairly crackled, and for not having the strength of mind to just walk away.

'Such as . . . ?' she prompted him.

'Such as why you found it necessary to come into my employ in disguise?'

She should have forced her feet to walk when she'd had the chance, she told herself, but it was too late now. He was leading her like a lamb to the slaughter back into the room, and sitting her down, with all the appearance of solicitousness, in the chair facing his across the wide expanse of desk.

This was it, then. This was the

moment she had been dreading; the moment that had been inevitable from the day she had accepted the challenge of this job, and done so under false pretences. It had seemed so harmless at the time; almost a game, really. But Alex was not a man who would take deceit lightly, and only now did Dana see what a very dangerous game she had been playing. Only now, as she faced the man who had against all odds come to mean so much to her, did she fully realise all that she had to lose.

7

Dana's breath seemed to be locked in her throat, and the words to explain her impulsive actions just wouldn't seem to come. She unclasped hands that were damp with nervous perspiration, and then had to resist the urge to smooth them along the silk of her skirt. She tried swallowing deeply, but still the words refused to present themselves, and helpless panic began to set in.

'I should start at the beginning if I were you,' Alex advised in an almost kindly tone, leaning back in his chair with a great show of patience and steepling his hands across his broad chest.

He had no right to look so relaxed and smug, Dana told herself, when it was he who had demanded the impossible. All she had tried to do was provide it.

'I was in the agency office helping out,' she began by way of explanation, 'when Jenny came in.'

'Jenny?' Alex stared at her blankly.

'The last employee before me,' Dana prompted, and nodded at the look on Alex's face that told her he remembered. 'She left here in tears and refused, absolutely, to come back. She said that after you, an ogre would be a doddle.'

'Did she?' He seemed more amused than annoyed.

Dana was beginning to get into the swing of things now. 'She was the last of a long line of secretaries to walk out on you. Your file at the agency,' she told him roundly, 'is inches thick.'

'I was never sent a single woman who was remotely suitable.' It was said as a statement of fact and could not in any way be mistaken for an excuse.

'There were no other complaints about their work.'

'Perhaps my standards are higher.'

Ooh! Dana held her temper rigidly in

check, and wondered how anyone could be so very sure that they were right and everyone else was wrong. 'Your biggest complaint,' she went on, trying to ignore the tiny smile that lurked around his mouth, 'seemed to be that they were too attractive, which had, in fact, absolutely nothing to do with their work.'

The smile, she was pleased to note, vanished at this. It had taken a while but she was finally getting somewhere.

'So,' he said, his voice suddenly dangerously quiet, 'what made you think that you could be what I needed?'

'I answered the phone when you rang. You may or may not remember, but I actually asked what you were looking for in a secretary.'

'If I'm so very hard to please,' he put in, 'why didn't you just tell me to take my business elsewhere?'

'Don't think I wasn't tempted,' Dana declared, leaning forward to glare at him. 'But if you recall, I did say that I was just helping out. It wasn't my place to tell you to get lost. I'll leave that

dubious pleasure to Gillian Spencer,'
she added, 'as it's her agency and you
are her client. I just didn't want to lose
a customer in her absence.'

'Are you even a secretary at all?'

'I trained as one, but I haven't
worked at all for two years. My
father — '

Her explanation was cut short as
Alex interrupted with a sneer, 'Obviously keeps you in style, judging by
your normal clothes. So you were just
amusing yourself by playing at being a
businesswoman.'

His calm assumption about the type
of person she was, was so wide of the
mark that his audacity quite took
Dana's breath away. Her first reaction
was to immediately correct him, but
then anger made her think again. He
had made his mind up, she told herself,
without knowing the very first thing
about her. Well, let him think whatever
he liked. She would tell him only how
she came to be in his employ and why
she had dressed the way she had; as for

anything else, she shrugged mentally and told herself firmly to forget it.

'I came,' she corrected him, 'only because no one else would. I dressed the way I did because you obviously wanted someone so dowdy that they could quite easily fade into the wallpaper. Dressing in my normal way might have prejudiced you against me even before you had given me a chance to show what I could do.'

'Am I so unreasonable?'

The question was a fair one, and she answered, equally fairly, 'I wouldn't really know. I've only been here for two weeks.'

'Have you been happy working for me?'

Another fair question, but she hesitated before answering, 'I wasn't happy about the deceit I had to practise, whatever you might think, but I did enjoy the work.' She knew that wasn't what he had meant, but it was the best that she could do.

'I should have known,' he said almost to himself, 'that no one could have that bad a taste in clothes.'

Dana risked a grin. 'Kerry, Gillian's secretary, obviously did, in what she calls her 'bigger days', but I do admit that they were pretty awful.'

'And if I hadn't come back early you'd have still been wearing them, and I'd have been none the wiser.' There was no answering smile; he still looked pretty grim.

'Well, you seemed pretty satisfied with the way things were. Why risk rocking the boat?' Dana paused for a brief moment before asking, 'What made you come back so soon?'

'The business was wrapped up sooner than I expected,' Alex said abruptly, as if he grudged the explanation.

It sounded plausible enough — so why did Dana have the distinct impression that he was lying, and wonder suddenly if that unexpected kiss could have had anything to do with his returning twenty-four hours earlier than planned? It was a ridiculous thought, but it somehow had her wishing that she could turn the clock back and still be the woman he had apparently been looking for. She longed foolishly for his approval, but she knew beyond any shadow of a doubt that the real Dana would never enjoy it. Not now, not ever. It was all over, and the only thing to do was leave and be grateful that her pride, at least, was still intact.

'If you would let Maggie know that I won't be here for lunch . . . ' She stood up, longing now for this to be over. It should have been so easy, walking away from this man and his unpredictable moods, but she knew it was going to be the hardest thing she had ever had to do. Somehow, amazingly, he was the one man she had ever really been seriously attracted to in all of her twenty-six years, and she was certain that under the arrogant shield he had built so carefully around himself was a man who would be very easy to love, and to go on loving.

'Where do you think you're going?'

Having turned to walk away, Dana

now turned abruptly back to face him. He hadn't moved so much as a muscle and still sat back in his chair, perfectly relaxed, and looking as if he didn't have a care in the world.

'I shall leave immediately, of course,' she told him now. 'I realise that you can't possibly want me to continue working for you under the circumstances.'

'Well,' he said smoothly, 'that's just where you're wrong, because it's exactly what I do want. You took on this job, for whatever reason, and it isn't finished yet. I expect you to stay until the work is completed.'

'But you can't . . . I won't . . . ' Dana thrashed about in a mental quagmire, feeling as if she were sinking into quicksand.

'But I can,' he returned forcefully, in a tone that brooked no argument, 'and you will, or your friend — Miss Spencer, isn't it? — will lose not only my custom but that of all the friends I was foolish enough to recommend her agency to.'

'You wouldn't.' Dana's tone lacked the conviction that she was striving for.

'Try me.' The two words were said most pleasantly, and they were even accompanied by a charming smile, but she didn't doubt for one minute that he meant them.

'Why? Why are you doing this? I'm quite obviously no different from all those other women — and now you know that, there's no point in my pretending any longer.'

'Ah,' he observed, 'but you *are* different, Dana, because you made yourself into the perfect secretary for me. And, that being the case, I don't intend to lose you now.'

It was all too much for Dana. She wanted to scream, she wanted to cry, but most of all she wanted to laugh. He didn't want to lose her. Those words could have meant so much, in different circumstances.

But she would stay. She really had no choice at all, did she? She had to stay for Gillian's sake, but most of all she had to stay for her own, because she wasn't ready, not yet, to kiss her impossible hopes and dreams goodbye.

★   ★   ★

'He knows, Kerry. He knows all about the way I deceived him — and he knows why.'

Dana held the receiver away from her endangered eardrums as Gillian's secretary shrieked, '*What?*'

'He found out last night,' she explained briefly. 'I gave in to temptation while he was away and went out as myself. Needless to say, he came back early.'

'Was he furious?'

Dana grinned wryly at the understatement and commented, 'You could say that.'

'Well, that's that, then.' Kerry sounded faintly relieved. 'You did your best and Gillian can't fault you for that. Did he throw you out on the spot? Is he going to sue us?'

'No, and no.' Dana laughed at the

other woman's blunt questions. 'Apparently I did my best so well that he wants to keep me there until the book is finished.'

'He must have liked my old clothes a lot.' Kerry sounded completely amazed. 'Do you have to keep wearing them as part of the job? He sounds a bit weird to me.'

'He's really not so bad.' Dana heard herself defending him, and wondered why she was bothering. 'I don't mind finishing the job. It's really quite interesting, and it'll be a lot easier now that I can be myself. I was always so afraid of being caught out.'

'I don't know if Gillian will be too happy about you working indefinitely for old Mean-and-Moody,' Kerry said doubtfully. 'He's not her favourite customer, you know, despite his useful contacts.'

'Then don't tell her,' Dana pleaded. 'It'll only be for another week or two. By the time the book is finished, Gillian will be back at the helm and we can all get back to normal.'

Normal! What was normal? Dana felt as if she just didn't know any more. She had barely got her grief over the death of her father into perspective before she was pitchforked into a wealth of other feelings that she was too inexperienced, even at her age, to either recognise or deal with in a way that made any sense.

She replaced the receiver thoughtfully and told herself, not for the first time, that she was a fool. A fool to have ever taken a job with the arrogant author in the first place, however strong her reasons for doing so, and a bigger fool not to have left his employment the minute she had known that she was attracted to the man.

Well, it was too late now. Alex was a man far too used to getting his own way, and having decided that he could not manage without her, he was going to make sure that she stayed to see the job through. If she didn't return to the house in the morning, Dana wouldn't put it past him to come and fetch her.

It was like looking at a stranger, Dana decided, staring at her reflection critically. A stranger who, while not a beauty, was certainly a vast improvement on the drab person she had become used to seeing over the last couple of weeks.

'Welcome back, Dana.' She nodded her approval at the trim figure dressed strikingly in a bright red suit. Wide grey eyes sparkled back at her, and she knew she had chosen the colour of her clothing for a purpose. She was the proverbial red rag today, and Mean-and-Moody Mitchell was the bull. He *would* notice her, she told herself stubbornly, and he would eventually be forced to admit that he was wrong — about women in general, and about her in particular.

He can't have it all his own way, she lectured herself constantly on the drive to his house. *He demanded that I stay, almost blackmailed me into doing so, and I shall insist that he treat me with proper respect. No shrieking at me one minute and stealing kisses the next.* She ignored the betraying shiver that stole along her spine and reminded herself, *It just won't do.*

Before leaving the car, she checked that her make-up wasn't smudged in any way, and was reassured as she walked towards the house by a distant, encouraging wolf-whistle from Adam. She acknowledged the sound with a brisk wave and, shoulders back and exuding confidence, she went inside.

If she'd been dressed in a sack, she told herself wrathfully, he'd have taken more notice. As it was, Alex barely acknowledged her arrival except by a grunted 'G'morning' and left the office the very minute he was able, disapproval stamped all over the back he kept so carefully turned her way.

I don't care. She slammed a filing cabinet drawer with unnecessary force and, as a result of her fury, she typed up twice as much material as she might normally have done in the time, and had every reason to be pleased with herself. 'I'll be glad if he stays permanently out of my way and just leaves me to it.' But the words sounded hollow, even to her own ears.

* * *

He was waiting for her on the following day, but any pleasure she might have felt at the sight of him was dispelled by his first furious words.

'You might think,' he said bitingly, 'that by working at fever pitch you'll be finished and out of here that much sooner. But that won't happen,' he went on sarcastically, 'if every page is littered with mistakes.'

Dana felt hot, embarrassed colour sweep across her high cheekbones, and she was barely able to stammer an apology. She had always prided herself on a job well done and couldn't for the life of her think how she had not noticed what must surely be a catalogue of errors, judging by Alex's behaviour.

157

It wasn't even as if he had been there breathing down her neck so that she could have blamed him for the distraction.

'I can't think how it happened,' she babbled, fighting for the composure that had deserted her in the face of his fierce criticism. 'I will, of course, work on this evening to make up any time spent doing corrections.'

He nodded coolly, as if he expected nothing less for the inconvenience she had so obviously caused him, and stalked from the room without another word.

Dana was close to tears as she sank into her chair and, spreading the sheets of manuscript out in front of her, she began to look for the blue circles that were the way Alex indicated mistakes. By the time she had finished, her eyes were dry and there was a scarlet mist in front of them.

'Littered with mistakes', to Dana, implied that there were a great many of them. But though she went thoroughly through the printed sheets, the thick blue circles pinpointed only two. Once brought up onto the computer screen, the corrections took only seconds, but she wasted a great many more fighting against the temptation to rise out of the chair and confront the author with all her righteously indignant guns blazing.

Deep breaths, she suddenly remembered reading, were a great way of calming a person down. She closed her eyes, breathed deeply, and gradually the red mist receded. It was what he wanted, she realised with a faint sense of shock, but going and confronting him would be playing right into his hands. Quite how she was so sure of that, she couldn't really say, but she knew without a doubt that she was right.

Opening her eyes again, Dana smiled; and, putting the corrected work to one side, she carried on with brisk efficiency from where she had left off the day before.

'It's gone eleven o'clock.'

She was proud that she didn't even

jump when the hand descended heavily onto her shoulder; but then, of course, she *had* been half-expecting it, and she removed the small headphones with a great show of reluctance. She looked up at Alex, carefully avoiding his eyes, and then she looked at her wristwatch. 'So it is,' she agreed pleasantly.

'Well, aren't you going to stop for coffee?' he asked with a trace of impatience in his tone.

'Oh, I don't think so.' She smiled sweetly and turned back to the screen. 'I'd rather make up the time I lost doing all those corrections.'

There was silence, and Dana could almost hear him battling with his conscience. She hid a smile and reached out for the headphones.

She was totally unprepared for the hand that suddenly captured her own, and for the feeling of warmth that threatened to swamp her as Alex's fingers entwined with hers. Very carefully, she kept her head down to hide the colour that had bloomed on her face in seconds.

Leaning forward until his mouth was level with her ear, Alex murmured, 'Okay. There weren't *that* many of them.'

'But you said . . . '

He sighed deeply, the warm breath stirring her hair and disturbing the calm that she had strived so hard to achieve. 'I know what I said. I was out of order.'

Dana turned around then and, staring carefully at the knot in Alex's silk tie, she enquired, 'Is that an apology?'

'It's whatever you want it to be.' Disconcertingly, he still held her hand, his fingers moving caressingly against the smooth skin of her knuckles. 'I shouldn't have spoken to you like that.'

'Taking pride in my appearance won't stop me from also taking pride in my work, you know,' she reminded him gently. 'I really am still the same Dana, despite the make-up and the changed hairstyle.'

'Are you?' There was almost a plea in the deep, questioning tone, as if he found it hard, even impossible, to believe. She knew she had to lighten the atmosphere. There was tension and temptation all around them, and Dana knew that if she looked into those hypnotic green eyes she would be lost. It was too soon, much too soon. She didn't even know what she wanted — and neither, she was sure, did he.

'I'm still the same Dana,' she managed with a light laugh, 'who finds it hard to resist Maggie's homemade biscuits.'

Alex chuckled, pulling her to her feet. The moment, to her relief and regret, had passed so swiftly that it left her wondering, as they made their way into Maggie's kitchen, if she'd simply imagined the whole thing.

8

There was calm, of a sort, as the days settled into an almost unvarying routine. Dana could sometimes manage to convince herself that she and Alex had become friends again, and on the surface they were. She watched him when his temper threatened to get the better of him and he wrestled to stifle a biting comment. She appreciated the very obvious effort he was making to behave with tact and diplomacy.

His behaviour made him much easier to be around, but somehow Dana missed the old bouts of verbal sparring that had kept her so much on her toes. She missed, too, the sparks those bouts had engendered, and the sizzling awareness that positively crackled between them with every confrontation.

This stranger — this well-behaved and excessively polite Alex — seemed afraid to act in any way that might be construed as over-familiar. He was always at great pains to keep a distance between them — and the wider the gap, the better, as far as Dana could tell.

Maggie, at least, wholeheartedly approved of the gentleman in their midst. 'You've changed him beyond all recognition,' she said in a pleased tone. 'He hasn't lost his temper for days.'

'I expect he's just pleased that the book is going so well,' Dana put in, unaccountably depressed at the thought that she might be responsible for the change in him — which was ridiculous, she told herself, because hadn't she always wanted him to be more human and approachable?

'Almost finished, is it?' Maggie asked, chopping carrots briskly. 'That must be a record. His agent will be pleased.'

'I wouldn't know; I've never met the man.'

She finished her coffee and rose reluctantly to her feet, to stand rooted to the spot as Maggie said cheerfully,

'Oh, she's a woman; didn't you know?'

'Isn't that where Alex stays when he has meetings in London?' The question was carefully casual, and no one could have dreamed what it cost Dana to ask it.

'Oh, yes.' Maggie was very matter-of-fact, not even bothering to look up as she added, 'They've had a very longstanding arrangement. It suits them both.'

'Yes.'

If Maggie hadn't been so busy, she might have wondered at Dana's small voice, and at the way she slipped from the room without another word.

Fool, Dana berated herself. *Fool, fool, fool.* She couldn't believe how naive she had been. Had she really thought that someone like Alex was just sitting there waiting with bated breath for someone like herself to happen along?

Yes. She laughed scornfully as she realised that it was just what she had thought. She had thought that he would suddenly see, as if scales had dropped from his eyes, that she was different. That she, unlike his mother and ex-wife, who had both deserted him, would never willingly leave him. She, who had known him for three short weeks, thought that she knew him better than people who had been in his life for years. Now, finally and bitterly, she was forced to acknowledge that she didn't know him at all, and that she never would.

Dana immediately and determinedly began to erect a barrier around herself: a shield from the hurt that she had laid herself wide open to when she was unwise enough to fall head over heels in love with the most unsuitable man she could ever have chosen.

She *was* in love with him; it was pointless now to deny it. Useless to tell herself that she couldn't possibly be, not in such a short space of time. She did love him, with a passion that surprised her — and because of the man he was, not in spite of it.

Well, she declared firmly, she had managed to live without that kind of love so far, and until now she hadn't felt that anything was missing from her life. Once she was out of Alex's house, away from the easy temptation to dream of what might have been, she would take stock of her life and, gathering up the pieces, fit them all back together in such a way that the one piece missing wouldn't even leave a hole.

Suddenly the end was in sight. The only thing left for Dana to do before the finished manuscript was printed up was to put in the last-minute changes that Alex had decided on. After that, this short and extraordinary episode in her life would be over. She tried hard to tell herself that she was glad.

'I can't believe how well you've done, Dana.'

Her heart lurched in the way that was becoming far too familiar to her, but Dana determinedly ignored the effect Alex's voice always seemed to have on her. It happened, she'd noticed, when he crept up on her unexpectedly, because if she had time to prepare herself she managed quite easily to compose herself and her feelings. She fought the urge now to tell him, not for the first time, to stop creeping up on her. It won't be for much longer, she reminded herself as she turned calmly to ask with a smile, 'What have I done so well?'

'Got my muddle of recordings, memory sticks, and notes so quickly into order.' He nodded approvingly. 'I'm such a messy worker, and I could never have pulled it all together without you. You know how I hate the mechanics of putting a book together. We make a great team, Dana.'

'It's nice of you to say so.' She tried, unsuccessfully, not to let his appreciation warm her, telling herself sternly that he would have said the same to any good secretary.

'Perhaps you'll come to the book launch,' he offered unexpectedly. 'I'd like you to be there. I really couldn't have done it without you.'

This was too much for Dana, suddenly finding praise heaped on praise, and from such a man. She had the awful feeling that in a moment she would disgrace herself and burst into the tears Alex hated so much. 'Nonsense,' she managed briskly. 'Any one of the other women could have done the same, had you given them half a chance.'

'We'll have to agree to differ on that,' he murmured darkly. 'Will you agree to come to London for the launch?'

His tone was persuasive, and Dana was sorely tempted, especially because he so obviously wanted her to be there. In her mind's eye she could see him with his arm protectively around her waist, introducing her to the people who were part of his successful author's life; the life he kept so ruthlessly separate from the one he lived here in the heart of the country. Not one person had visited or even called in since Dana had been working there. Not even, she realised with a start, the agent whose house he so often shared in London.

The sudden thought was like a dash of cold water in her face, and she almost gasped aloud. What on earth was she thinking about, that she could let herself be tempted into facing the woman who belonged in Alex's life? It was bad enough that she had fallen in love with the man; but to allow herself to be hurt still further and to drag out the goodbyes that were inevitable was the act of a bigger idiot than Dana intended to be. *Just let go*, she advised herself. *It really is the only way.*

'I don't think that's such a good idea, do you?' she said aloud. 'I expect it'll be several months away, and I could be anywhere by then. It'd be silly to make promises that I might not be able to keep.'

She watched the brilliant green of his eyes harden to emerald ice and ruthlessly suppressed a shiver, telling herself that he couldn't have it all, that it wasn't fair for him to expect her to be on call just because he liked her secretarial skills.

'Are you telling me,' he said, scowling, 'that you're going to just walk out of here the minute the book is finally wrapped up, and that will be that?'

'That's about the size of it.' She managed to keep her tone firm and even. 'I came here to do a job, and that job is very nearly complete. I have to get back to my own life.'

'Ah, yes.' Alex nodded with a sneer on his lips that twisted Dana's heart, and made her wonder at the way his approval had vanished so swiftly. 'Of course. You're not really a business-woman, are you? Just 'helping out', I seem to remember. So what's it to be next? Another holiday to top up the tan, or won't Daddy run to that?'

Dana rounded on him in a fury, telling herself that not knowing of her father's death was no excuse; he had no right to judge her without knowing any of the facts, no right at all. 'You leave my father out of this. What I do or where I go has absolutely nothing to do with you.'

His expression was bleak as he admitted slowly, 'Of course, you're right. The fact escaped me for a moment, but I won't forget again.' And turning, he left the room without another word, slamming the door with an almighty crash that vibrated off the walls.

Dana thought that she would never forget the look in his eyes. He had looked — she searched for the word — defeated. But that was ridiculous. Alex had everything that money could buy, and a woman in his life. Why should he be so upset because he didn't have the secretary of his choice on tap? Even he couldn't have *everything* his own way.

The day couldn't come quickly enough for Dana when she could walk out of the beautiful thatched house and, hopefully, never have to come back. She felt that she had done all that she could for both Gillian and Alex, and she refused to do more. All she wanted was time to herself, time to get her own life back into some semblance of order. Yet she found herself making so many excuses to prevent herself from leaving. She reprinted page after page of manuscript. She didn't know if Alex noticed, but if he did he was very careful not to comment on the matter, and for that she was grateful.

Of course, Dana knew quite well that she couldn't go on pretending indefinitely, and that the moment of truth couldn't be put off much longer. Alex was, thankfully, in London, because she didn't think she would be able to say goodbye to him and keep her composure. The awareness that he was very probably with his agent helped her to make the decision that it really was time to leave. While he was in the house with her and Maggie, it was too easy to pretend that there was no one else in his life; that at any moment he might discover that Dana was actually all that he wanted in a woman.

'Today should see it all finally finished,' Dana told Maggie over her morning coffee, 'and if there are any last-minute changes, well, I'm sure that Alex can manage them himself or suffer a short visit from someone from the agency.'

She was so busy concentrating on keeping her voice steady that she barely glanced at the older woman as she spoke. Instead, she peered into her coffee cup and swirled the liquid round and round with the teaspoon. It was like a mini-whirlpool, and it mirrored the way she had felt ever since she had fallen so unadvisedly in love with Alex. She had been spun round and round, in a fever of wanting and wishing, and the threat of being sucked under by the force of her love was very real. She had to leave while she still had the strength to do so, and she knew it.

'So you're really going?' There was a question in Maggie's voice — as if, thought Dana fancifully, she actually had a choice. She even wondered for a moment if Maggie knew how she felt about Alex, but then she dismissed the idea. Maggie added, almost wistfully, 'We shall miss you.'

'Oh, Maggie, I'll miss you, too.' Dana jumped up to hug the woman, and admitted to herself that she had become very fond of her. It had been a long time since anyone had mothered her, and she had thoroughly enjoyed the experience while it lasted. She kissed the plump cheek, and only as she drew away did she notice that Maggie's usual rosy complexion was noticeably paler and, under the fine lines of age, the features were drawn, the blue eyes lacking in their usual brightness.

'Are you all right, Maggie?' She heard her own voice sharpen with sudden concern. 'You're looking very tired.'

The older woman dismissed her anxiety. 'Oh, it's just a bit of a cold. I'll be fine. Just mind you don't catch it, now.'

Dana allowed herself to be shooed out of the kitchen, but the disquiet, once acknowledged, could not be dismissed so easily. Alex should know that his housekeeper wasn't well, and she decided to tell him as soon as he returned — and then realised that she wouldn't be there when he did.

She resisted the urge to check on Maggie, knowing she wouldn't appreciate being fussed over, being as touchy as she was about her age and about it being blamed for any ailments that might occur. She would leave a note for Alex, she decided eventually, and keep her eye on Maggie discreetly for the rest of the day.

Somehow she couldn't leave it, though, and only minutes later Dana found herself making her way silently back to the kitchen, feverishly searching for an excuse for going there that wouldn't let Maggie know she was checking up on her.

The crash, when it came, didn't even surprise her. It was almost as if she had been expecting it, or something like it. She broke into a run, throwing open the door so that it bounced against the wall with a crash.

Maggie stood white-faced, gripping the table and staring in horror at the shards of china scattered all around her feet. Before Dana could reach her, she broke into dry, heartbroken sobs. 'It's one of the best pieces.' She lifted a shaking hand to her forehead in a telling gesture, and then she seemed to go limp.

Dana reached her before she actually fell. 'Put your arm round my neck, Maggie. Let's get you to a chair.'

Maggie seemed to slump rather than sit, and all that energy she normally exuded appeared to have melted clean away. Dana noticed the grey tinge to her complexion with growing concern. An unhealthy pallor was a sure sign that all was not well, and it was something that Dana was too familiar with to dismiss lightly. Glancing from the kitchen window, she saw to her relief that Adam was working within shouting distance. A quick look at Maggie reassured her that the older woman was not in any immediate danger of falling from the chair.

'Don't move,' she ordered, and running outside, she yelled at the top of her voice and gestured wildly the minute Adam looked her way. He seemed to stare at her for an awfully long time, but even in her distress Dana was sure that it was only seconds before he was racing towards her.

'What is it? What's wrong?'

He was calling while he was still yards away, and Dana placed a finger to her lips before saying when he was close enough to hear her low tone, 'It's Maggie. She seems very sick, Adam. I think she should be in bed, and I can't manage alone.'

'Just tell me what you want me to do.'

She liked the way he didn't waste more time on questions, and he helped her to get Maggie into bed before ringing for the doctor without further instruction.

'How did you know who to ring?' Dana asked him, impressed and curious all at the same time.

He grinned. 'In a village of this size there's only the one doctor. He'll be here in five minutes.'

★   ★   ★

'How can I stay in this bed?' Maggie fretted, mangling the neat grey curls as she turned her head this way and that on the pillow.

'You'll do as the doctor told you.' The stern tone was alien to Dana, but she forced herself to use it. 'You heard what he said. You have a severe case of flu, and if you don't rest you'll very likely end up in hospital.'

'But who will — '

'I will — whatever it was you were going to say,' Dana insisted. 'Now, will you rest, or do I have to tie you to the bed?'

It was a long time before she settled, and Dana was even beginning to

179

wonder if she would have to carry out her threat before Maggie's eyelids finally began to droop. She tried not to think too hard about whether she was glad or sorry that her departure had to be delayed.

'She mustn't be left alone.' They were the doctor's very words. But Adam could just as easily have stayed; he had actually offered to do so. How swiftly Dana had insisted that Maggie would feel better if it was she who stayed; that it would be better if she had another woman looking after her — though of course, she would appreciate Adam's offer.

Guilt might have something to do with it, Dana was forced to admit, because if she hadn't been so wrapped up in her own problems she would have noticed days before that Maggie wasn't her usual self. How could she have taken her so for granted? she berated herself. A woman who had shown her so much kindness, once she had accepted her presence in the house, and had made her feel like a part of the family — every bit as cherished as Alex had always been.

Wrapping herself in one of Maggie's voluminous aprons, Dana set to and swept up the pieces of china. She looked more closely. No, not china, but an oven-proof casserole by the look of the bits. A peep in the fridge confirmed it, as all of the ingredients were to hand for what was obviously the evening meal.

I'll make it for her. Dana nodded, pleased to be able to find some way of passing the time and helping Maggie in the process. It was obvious to her from the amount of meat and vegetables that Maggie had been expecting Alex home. She shivered and then refused to think about him again, firmly telling herself that it was Maggie who needed her now, and that Alex had nothing to do with it.

She took another look in at the house-keeper before she started on the meal, and was quite frightened at how frail she looked. Maggie was one of those women whose age was quite hard to determine, but if Dana had been asked, she would have placed her quite confidently somewhere in her mid-sixties. Looking at her lying so still now, tucked up in the bed, Dana thought she looked more like a woman in her late seventies.

She wasn't doing this for Alex's sake, she assured herself as she chopped vegetables furiously, but only because it would please Maggie and stop her worrying about her precious charge starving while she was confined to bed.

He didn't deserve to be worried and fretted over the way he was, as far as Dana was concerned. He had been in Maggie's company just as much as she herself had, she reminded herself bitterly, *and* had known her for a great many more years. It should have been obvious to him days ago that his housekeeper was not her usual self. The fact that she was so sick now could be laid squarely at his door, and so Dana planned tell him the minute he came in.

Peeling and slicing onions was the

reason Dana gave to herself for the tears that began to course slowly and steadily down her face, to drip — unhygienically, she was sure — onto the vegetables. In truth, though, the tension of the day had all become too much to bear. The thought of leaving Alex forever, coupled with Maggie's sudden and unexpected collapse, was forcing her to shed the tears that were so foreign to her nature.

It was just as well, Dana admitted as she went along to Maggie's bedroom for the umpteenth time, that the housekeeper's apartment was conveniently close to the kitchen, with her bedroom and bathroom set behind the cosy sitting room that Dana had visited before.

The worried blue gaze flew to her face the minute she stepped inside the door. 'I must get up,' trembled Maggie from colourless lips.

'You'll do no such thing,' Dana told her calmly. 'The doctor said you're to stay in bed until you're *completely* better.' She emphasised the word 'completely', but didn't raise her voice or allow her tone to sharpen, not wanting Maggie to see how worried she was.

The veined hands twitched incessantly at the sheets. 'But there's Alex's meal to get. I've never let him down . . . '

'And you won't tonight,' Dana assured her, tactfully refraining from reminding the sick woman that Alex was quite capable of feeding himself should the need arise. 'There's a casserole in the oven. I found all the ingredients in the fridge. I expect you can smell it if you try hard enough.'

She knew she had said the right thing when she saw the strained look ease on Maggie's face, and the hint of a smile curve her mouth as she whispered, 'Thank you, dear. I should have known I could count on you.' High praise indeed from someone who had spent most of her life being relied upon by others, and one other in particular.

Suddenly, that one other in particular

came hurrying into the room, and sent every thought Dana had clean out of her head.

'What is it? What's wrong?' There was no doubting the anxiety in his worried tone. 'Have you hurt yourself, Maggie? Was it an accident? What's happened?'

Dana was angry all over again when she watched Maggie struggling to sit up. Trust him to come barging in. Had he no sense at all? Just when she had Maggie nicely calmed down, in he came, immediately undoing all of her good work.

Standing up herself, she pressed a hand onto the older woman's shoulder, almost forcing her back down under the covers, and saying as she did so, 'Maggie had a bit of a turn brought on by the flu, and the doctor has ordered her to stay in bed until she's quite better.' She fixed him with a fierce glare and shook her head just once as she tried to convey that he should ask no more questions until they were out of the room.

'It's just foolishness,' Maggie tried to deny, but there was no real conviction in her weak tone. 'I shall be up tomorrow, never you fear.'

'I won't hear of it.' Alex was obviously adamant, and Dana was, for once, pleased with him. 'You'll do as you're told, or you'll have me to deal with.'

'But who'll look after you?' Maggie's voice was high and anxious. 'How can I rest when there's no one to take care of you and this house?'

'I can take . . . ' he began, but was given no chance to finish.

'No,' the housekeeper interrupted querulously, 'I won't hear of it.'

She was clearly getting agitated, and Alex hurried to reassure her. 'All right, Maggie, I'll get someone from the village to come in until you're better.'

'Strangers,' she said, sounding horrified, 'poking around in my kitchen? Oh, no! I don't mean to be difficult, but I really think I shall be all right by tomorrow, and Dana has already seen to your meal for tonight.'

Dana and Alex shared a look, and Alex shrugged lightly and raised his dark eyebrows expressively as if asking Dana for suggestions, because he was at a complete loss.

'Is there anyone that you would accept?' Dana took Maggie's hand. 'Perhaps your sister,' she suggested helpfully.

'She wouldn't do.' The grey head shook fretfully, and then was still as her blue gaze fixed thoughtfully onto Dana's concerned face. Dana saw the trap yawning and she knew exactly what was coming before the words were spoken.

'But *you* would, Dana.' Maggie's fingers curled round her hand, holding her a prisoner as surely as if she were tied to a ball and chain. 'I can trust you, and I would promise to stay in bed as long as you wanted me to if you were here. Please stay — for me.'

Two faces watched her expectantly — waiting, she knew, for her answer. But they all knew there was only one answer that she could, in all conscience, give.

'I'll stay,' she said simply, and wondered at the surge of elation that rushed through her body like a high-voltage electrical charge. She had never truly wanted to leave.

9

'This is delicious,' Alex approved as he helped himself to another serving of casserole.

'You needn't sound so surprised.' Dana found that her own appetite, and her usually dependable powers of social chit-chat, had deserted her. She was all too well aware of the fact that if it hadn't been for Maggie's illness, she wouldn't be in the house at all. Not sitting there at the kitchen table watching Alex eat the food that she had prepared, with every appearance of enjoyment. Nor would she have been battling to subdue the warm feeling that the sight of him, and just being in his company, gave her. Did he think that she was pushy, taking over the way that she had? It seemed not, as his next words were spoken in genuine appreciation of all she had done.

'Anyone would have done the same,'

she was in a hurry to point out.

'No,' he denied emphatically, 'anyone would not have done the same. A lot of people I know would have said it was none of their business and gone on their way without a backward glance.'

'They wouldn't!' Dana couldn't really believe that. Her experience of people was obviously very different from what his must have been, she thought.

'Indeed they would,' he insisted, his green eyes dark and unfathomable, 'and I do realise that Maggie put you on the spot in there. This was to have been your last day with us, wasn't it?'

She nodded without speaking, and tried very hard indeed not to actually be *glad* that Maggie was ill and obviously needed her, thereby giving her a genuine reason for staying. *I really don't wish you to be ill, Maggie.* The words ran silently through Dana's head as if she were saying them to the sick woman herself. *But, now that you are, I want to thank you so much for asking me to stay.*

'Please don't feel obliged to change your own plans.' Alex sounded very polite and correct. He went on, 'I realise that you have to get back to your own life, and I can easily find someone in the village to take over, in spite of Maggie's strenuous objections.'

Dana realised that her own words were being thrown back at her. He didn't want her to stay, she was forced to acknowledge, and was trying to make it easy for her to turn her back on the promise she'd made so recently to Maggie. She almost said that, yes, she would prefer to leave, but something held her back. She glanced across the table at him and found him watching her expectantly, as if he already knew her answer. He probably thought that he did.

She swallowed deeply, and then said in her firmest tone, 'I won't be going anywhere until Maggie is better.'

If she hadn't been staring straight at him, she might have missed the fleeting expression in his eyes. He was surprised, that much was very plain, but there was something else. Relief? Pleasure? Impossible, she told herself; the only reason he could possibly have for either of those things was that she had saved him the job of looking for someone else to temporarily fill Maggie's shoes.

'Unless, of course, you *want* me to go?' The words had come from nowhere, and she was horrified. It was almost as if she were testing him and now he was the one put on the spot.

'I never did.' He was looking at her in the strangest way, and for a long moment she forgot to breathe as she stared, mesmerised, into the deep green of his eyes. 'It's as if you belong here,' he laughed hoarsely, 'in all your different guises. Isn't that the most ridiculous thing?'

'Ridiculous,' she agreed huskily, and was filled with a warmth that had nothing at all to do with the central heating, or with the casserole that she had barely tasted. 'I'll just check on Maggie.' She jumped up, feeling that she had to move away and break the spell that held them with gossamer strands. She almost flew from the room.

The older woman hadn't eaten very much from the tray that Dana had so carefully prepared, but she was relieved to note that Maggie's colour was definitely better, and she was looking far less tense than she had earlier.

'I couldn't manage very much,' she whispered apologetically, catching at Dana's hand as she reached for the tray, 'but you did very well, dear, very well indeed.'

Dana removed the tray to a side table and returned to sit beside the bed, patting Maggie's hand as she did so. The older woman needed reassurance that they would manage without her undoubted skills in the kitchen, that much was apparent, and Dana didn't intend to leave the room until Maggie was quite happy with the arrangements. It would be crucial to her recovery that she shouldn't be worrying about her beloved Alex, because to have her lying there fretting could only prolong the healing process, Dana was quite sure.

'I have a long way to go to match your culinary efforts in any way,' she said with a grin, 'but he won't starve while I'm in the kitchen, I promise you.'

Maggie sighed deeply and sank back into her pillows. 'You're a good girl, Dana,' she said, nodding. 'Just what's needed. Just what's always been needed.'

It was a funny thing to say, and Dana only hoped that Maggie didn't have any ideas about grooming her as an apprentice housekeeper. This was a one-off, she told herself, and it was the last time that she was going to take on a job she wasn't specifically trained for, simply because she was available when a vacancy came up. What that man really needed, as was becoming increasingly apparent, was a wife to see that his life ran along the smoothly oiled wheels that he so obviously required in his profession as a writer. That, Dana reminded herself, was one job that would never be hers. She had neither the qualifications nor the desire for that particular career, and it would be as well if she stopped trying to convince herself that she had.

'A cup of tea, Maggie?' she offered as she stood up. 'Or would you prefer a cup of coffee, perhaps?'

The grey head shook emphatically. 'They'll keep me awake . . . But if I could have a cup of the malted drink — it's in the cupboard — that would help me to sleep.'

Dana's nose twitched as she carried the tray into the kitchen and was met by the fragrant aroma of freshly ground coffee. She sniffed appreciatively and then looked around, allowing her mouth to form into a round 'O' of surprise. 'You,' she said sternly, 'are not the helpless man that Maggie would have me believe.'

'I can load a dishwasher and make a pot of coffee. Why, I've even been known to cook the odd omelette on occasion.' Alex took the tray from Dana and smiled down at her ruefully. 'But don't tell her that, or she'll swear that redundancy is looming.'

'You mean,' said Dana knowingly, 'that she needs you as much as you need her?'

Alex shrugged. 'She's been a mother to me. How can you pension off a mother? I just wish that she would accept some help in the house. I know it's too much for her to manage at her age, but she's so stubborn, and she resists my every attempt at making life easier for her.' He sighed. 'This is my fault — her illness. I should have seen it coming.'

'Nonsense.' Dana found herself denying the blame that she had, just hours previously, heaped on his head. 'I saw the way she refused to accept help from the village. I'm surprised she accepted mine.'

'I'm not.' Alex turned from his task of clearing Maggie's tray and he smiled so warmly, so approvingly, that Dana felt her toes curl with pleasure inside her shoes. *Just stop it*, she warned herself. *You know the power he has over you, and that he exerts it to get his own way, yet you fall for it every time. You really should have more sense.*

Easy to say, she acknowledged, but so hard to heed. Especially when Alex was standing so close that she could feel his warm breath lifting tendrils of her hair. She concentrated on making Maggie's drink, using every bit of her willpower to ignore the man watching her so closely and the goose bumps of awareness that disturbed the smooth flesh of her arms.

'Is there anything that you don't know how to do?' The question, coming from a man of Alex's talents, surprised Dana, though she tried hard not to show it.

I don't know how to make you love me, she admitted silently. Aloud, she said, 'I couldn't write a book, and . . . oh, lots of other things.' She lifted the milky drink, prepared in Maggie's favourite cup. 'I'll just take this through.'

'I'll do that.' Alex's fingers brushed her own as he took the cup from her hand. Was it intentional? Dana didn't really think so, and yet to her oversensitive imagination it felt amazingly like a caress. 'You relax and drink your coffee,' he added.

The door had barely swung to behind him when there was a sharp rap on the glass of the back door. The sound was so sudden and unexpected that Dana dropped the spoonful of brown sugar that had been destined for her cup. Tutting at the gritty mess, she hurried to the door and, wrenching impatiently at the door handle, came face to face with Adam.

'Oh, it's you,' she said. 'Come on in quickly; you're letting the cold air in. You made me jump and I've spilled sugar everywhere. Coffee?'

'Love one.' He sat down, explaining as he did so, 'I thought I'd just check how Maggie was doing, and if you needed any more help.'

Dana sat down opposite him. 'Maggie will be fine — if we can convince her to rest. I'll take a rain check for the help. I just might need to call on you, as I'll be the one doing Maggie's job for a few days.'

Adam looked impressed. 'She really has taken to you, hasn't she? She'd never let the boss' ex-wife within a mile of her kitchen.'

Dana's ears pricked up at the rare mention of the Thatches' former mistress, but she dared not encourage further confidences, conscious as she was that Alex might return at any moment. Instead, she carefully steered the conversation onto more solid ground. After the tension she felt whenever Alex was around, Dana found it remarkably pleasant to be able to relax again in a man's company. In no time she found herself chatting away and even swapping recipes with Adam who, it turned out, was something of a frustrated chef and liked nothing better than to experiment in the kitchen.

They were laughing uproariously about his 'curry special' that could be relied on, he had informed her with a straight face, to take the roof from your mouth even before it had touched your tongue, when Dana became aware that Alex had come into the room and taken up a stance just inside the doorway, watching them through narrowed green eyes with an expression on his face that looked suspiciously like disapproval. Perhaps he disapproved of them laughing when Maggie was so sick, Dana thought, and guilt immediately wiped the smile from her lips and the merriment from her eyes.

Red-faced and flustered, she began to explain. 'Oh, Alex, Adam just popped in to see how Maggie was, and to offer his services if we needed any help.'

'I see. Very kind of him.'

He sounded polite enough, but Dana could see the hostility practically oozing from his every pore, and her guilt was rapidly replaced by hot anger. What right had he, she asked herself furiously, to sit in judgement over what was, after all, just a harmless joke at no one's expense, when he hadn't even noticed that his own housekeeper was ill? Why, if it hadn't been for her and Adam, the result might have been much more serious.

'It *was* kind of him,' Dana said, raising her face so that she could glare at him and try to make him see how rude he was being. 'I couldn't have managed without Adam's help when Maggie collapsed.'

'It was a good thing you were close by.' Alex eventually endeavoured to inject a hint of warmth into his tone, and he managed to unbend enough to pour them and himself more coffee and join them at the table.

'I wasn't actually that close,' Adam said with a grin. 'It's just that Dana has a very good set of lungs. I'm pretty sure they must have heard her in Salisbury.'

Laughing, Dana reached out to slap him but missed as he ducked to one side. 'You'll feel my good left hook if I get any more of your sauce, young man!'

Alex smiled at their banter, but she thought the green eyes still held a hint of disapproval. Shrugging mentally, she determined to ignore it and forced herself to chat easily to Adam until he finished his coffee and eventually left, renewing his offer of help as he did so.

'Wasn't that nice of him?' Dana said.

Ignoring her smiling comment, Alex said in belligerent tones, 'He seemed very at home in my kitchen.'

Dana stared at him and he glared back ferociously as if, she thought fancifully, it were somehow her fault that Adam had called at all, though why it should be wrong for the young man to visit she was at a loss to understand. She carefully bit back the angry retort that trembled on the tip of her tongue and said evenly, 'He probably quite often has his elevenses in here with Maggie. She seems to be very fond of him.'

'She's not the only one.'

There was no mistaking his meaning this time, and Dana's temper began to climb steeply as she asked bitingly, 'What's that supposed to mean?'

Alex's chin jutted. 'Whatever you want it to.'

Just why he was behaving like a spoilt child, Dana couldn't begin to work out, and she decided there and then that she wasn't even going to begin to try. 'We had this conversation,' she began, 'or one very like it, only a matter of days ago. It was ridiculous then, and even more so now, in view of Adam's kindness and the fact that his visit was prompted by concern over Maggie's health. If you have a problem with your gardener's conduct, I suggest you take it up with him and stop making snide suggestions about him behind his back.' She spun furiously on her heel, but had taken only two steps when Alex's voice, the tone low and apologetic, stopped her in her tracks.

'Don't go. I really have no problem with Adam's conduct, only with my own.' He came to stand in front of Dana, resting his hands lightly on her shoulders and looking seriously down into her eyes. 'Why is it that around you

I forget that I'm a grown man, and find myself behaving like a jealous schoolboy?'

At his touch and his words, hope spiralled and soared. Alex, jealous? Of Adam? Surely not. 'But . . . why?' Dana managed to ask.

'You looked so damn cosy with him, so at ease. You're never like that with me. I thought we were friends . . . '

Friends? He wanted to be friends. But she wanted — hoped — for so much more. 'Sometimes — ' she began, and then corrected herself in a brittle tone. 'No, always — you ask too much of me, Alex. I can't be all things to you.'

The hands cupping her shoulders moved smoothly, caressingly, down her arms, and the movement sent awareness sizzling through her body and longing through her soul.

'But you're wrong,' he murmured. 'So wrong — because I think that you could very easily be everything to me.'

She was drawn into his arms, into the warmth of his body, and there was no hesitation, no thought of drawing back, because she knew that whatever Alex wanted in a woman was what she wanted to be. What he needed, she would become, without fear or hesitation.

* * *

If it hadn't been for the untimely interruption of Maggie's voice calling fretfully, would Alex have declared his love for her? Dana shivered slightly, recalling the look in his eyes as he had, with great reluctance, released her.

'This,' he had assured her with great emphasis, 'is only the beginning for us. I can't fight what I feel, and I'm finding that I no longer want to try.'

Her smile widened as she realised that somehow she had managed to overcome his reservations; that perhaps against his better judgement, and probably against his will, she could make him love again. Dana hoped that whatever lay in the way of the happiness they would eventually share, it would be set aside — and that included ex-wives and ex-lovers. At any moment now, she was sure, he would come laughing into the room, take her into his arms and kiss all her doubts away. This was the first day of the rest of their lives, full of promises, dreams and wishes that could all hopefully come true.

Dana wielded the floor mop enthusiastically in the sunny kitchen, determined that Maggie would find no fault when her health improved. After all, if it hadn't been for Maggie . . .

'What on earth do you think you're doing?'

She hadn't heard the back door open and Dana spun round, very conscious of the comical picture she must present, wrapped as she was almost from head to toe in one of Maggie's voluminous floral pinafores. In the doorway, an irate expression on her pretty face and with her fair curls practically bristling, stood the familiar figure of her best and closest friend.

'Gillian! You're back.' Dana couldn't

hide her delight.

'And in the nick of time, it seems.' The petite blonde stepped into the kitchen and closed the door behind her with a sharp click. 'Look at you. Just look.' She waved a hand in Dana's direction with a disparaging flourish. 'Secretarial work for someone of your talents is bad enough, but scrubbing floors . . . Just who does that damn man think he is?'

'But he — ' Dana protested urgently.

But she knew immediately that she was wasting her breath as Gillian went on furiously, 'He's been a fly in the agency's ointment from the first day he walked into my office. Enough is well and truly enough. He's gone too far. It's obviously a Jack-of-all-trades he wants, not one of my highly trained women — and certainly not you.'

'He didn't — '

'Think that I'd find out?' Gillian nodded derisively. 'I'll just bet that he didn't.' The usually bubbly blonde was like a river in full flood. There was no stopping the tumbling flow of words and no chance at all of getting a word in edgewise, try as Dana might. She could see the other woman's point of view. As far as Gillian was concerned, Dana was being exploited by one of her clients, and while she was doing her a favour into the bargain. It was really no wonder that she was so annoyed. *I'll let her have her say and get it out of her system,* she decided, *and then I can put her right.*

' . . . an interior designer of your experience,' Gillian rushed on, 'dressed like Mrs Mop. Your father would turn in his grave, Dana. Kerry said that you were going to teach him a lesson, but I never dreamed you'd attempt anything like this. What are you doing? Making yourself indispensable to the man so that you can eventually drop him flat?'

Dana opened her mouth to hotly deny the accusation as her friend paused for breath, but before her denial could be uttered, a deep voice, icily polite, spoke from behind her.

'So,' Alex said grimly, 'that was the object of the exercise, was it? And the funny thing is, you very nearly succeeded. Isn't that hilarious?'

10

The confrontation between the two people that Dana loved most in the world, and the bitter words exchanged, had been a shocking blur to her. She could only watch helplessly as between them they tore her dreams into shreds of futile might-have-beens. She felt that there was nothing she could say in her own defence, even had she been able to halt the hot vitriolic flow, because she was only too aware that at the very beginning she *had* been going to teach Alex what she saw as a well-deserved lesson.

Now Dana curled up in her small bed like a wounded animal in its burrow. She didn't cry, because she knew it was far too late for tears and regrets. She didn't have to look at her bedside clock to know that time still marched on for everyone, leaving memories, good and bad, in its wake. If she allowed herself just one regret, it would be for the pain she had caused Alex by encouraging him to trust again. He would see hers as the final betrayal; the final proof that attractive women were, indeed, all the same.

She wished she could have told him that he was wrong. Instead, she had said nothing, allowing Gillian to usher her from the house, managing only to murmur 'Maggie?' at the very last moment. Alex's scathing 'We shall be fine' had cut Dana to the quick. He didn't add 'without you' — but the words were there, thick in the silence.

Once in the car, Gillian fumed all the way back to Bournemouth about men in general and the one they had just left in particular. Dana let the one-sided conversation flow over and round her, just longing for the nightmare to be over.

'I had to bring you away.' Gillian only looked at Dana, really looked, when she was parked in front of the building that housed Dana's small flat. 'You do see that?'

Dana supposed she could have told her then; tried to make her understand that all had not been as Gillian appeared to see it. She even took a breath in anticipation, and then she let it out in a deep sigh, because it hardly seemed worth the effort when there would be so little purpose in a confession of that sort.

She had been glad when Gillian finally left. For once they were completely out of step with one another, and her friend's firmly voiced conviction that black was black and Alexander Mitchell was blackest of all, together with her endless fussing and good advice, only served to drain away the little energy Dana had left.

Perhaps Gillian was right, she thought tiredly. She had, after all, known the man longer than Dana had. But only in a business capacity, a tiny voice inside her head insisted on reminding her. Only she herself, it would seem, had caught glimpses of the real Alex — the one hidden so carefully behind the arrogant and often rude exterior. Glimpses, she realised now, were all that he had ever allowed. Getting him to talk about himself had been like pulling teeth without an anaesthetic, and he had rarely shown that much interest in her own background. On reflection, she decided, though he had accused her of misleading him, it was in fact his own lack of curiosity that had led to any misunderstandings between them. She had never actually lied, and she knew that she wouldn't have done so.

Dana sighed heavily and brooded on why life had to be so complicated for some people. Most fell in love at some time in their lives. The majority married and lived happily ever after, or they divorced and tried again, and they made it all look relatively simple. She sighed again. If only it could be for her.

Hours later she was still huddled under the quilt and no nearer a solution. She had two clear choices, and they both beckoned, but neither of them was an easy one.

The first was to forget him — put Alexander Mitchell out of her mind and out of her life. It was a simple solution, and the first steps had already been taken. All she had to do, she told herself, was to keep busy; throw herself into the career that still held a fascination for her, even after so long away — back into the work that she was trained for — and eventually she would surely get over him.

She had almost convinced herself that she could do it, and perhaps she would have actually succeeded, if only Alex's good-looking face hadn't appeared so clearly, etched onto her closed eyelids. Her eyes flew open, but the movement failed to dispel the illusion, and Dana found herself studying the square jut of his jaw; the warm, full curve of his mouth; the black head of crisply curling hair; and the green glint of eyes that mirrored all the emotions that he tried so hard to hide.

A complicated man? Yes, he was, and

she couldn't deny it. But he was the first man she had truly loved, and something told Dana that he would be her only love. For all his faults, or perhaps even because of them, he was the man she wanted; and she finally admitted that she couldn't give up on him — not yet. Not without a fight. And that — she smiled grimly — was her second solution.

* * *

'You can't be serious?' Gillian was horrified. 'He's awful, Dana. Forget him, and find yourself a sane and sensible guy.'

For a fleeting moment Dana wondered why she was bothering to try to win Gillian over because, with or without her friend's blessing, she meant to try again with Alex. He knew there was something special between them, and all she had to do was force him to admit it and give it a chance to thrive.

'I love him, Gill,' she said honestly,

'and I want him. Not some sane and sensible guy who would probably bore me rigid within two minutes of the marriage being blessed. Now, are you for me, or are you against me?'

She watched her friend hesitate — almost saw her wrestle with her conscience — and she knew that in her place she would feel exactly the same. Gillian only wanted what she thought was best for Dana. But when it came down to it, it wasn't Gillian's place to choose. Would she be willing to admit that? Dana found that she was holding her breath as she waited for a reply that could make or break their friendship.

'I was wrong on both counts.' Gillian smiled and put out her hand. 'He must be quite a guy. I wish you all the luck in the world. Not that you need it. He doesn't stand a chance in the face of such grim determination. I'll book the church, shall I, and get measured for the bridesmaid's dress?'

They laughed, Dana grasped her friend's hand, and the tension that had been steadily building between them dissolved in a moment like ice in the sun. 'Thanks, Gill.'

'I didn't do anything except make matters a whole lot worse,' Gillian protested. 'If I hadn't come bursting in on you in my heavy-handed way, you'd still be there now.'

Dana shook her head. 'We weren't being straight with each other, Alex and I,' she admitted slowly, her face serious. 'And I don't think that love can really survive unless honesty is at its core. I have to know the real Alex, warts and all, and he has to know the real me.'

But first, Dana acknowledged, she had to come up with a plan to get them back together. Only once Alex had admitted that he couldn't live without her — and he would, she intended to make sure of it — could they begin to lay a solid foundation to support the love that had materialised so unexpectedly. Only then could they build on it.

Having mentioned her desire to know more about the man she loved, Dana was surprised and delighted when Gillian wholeheartedly applauded the scheme and suddenly produced not only half a dozen of Alex's books, but a handful of his press cuttings as well. Gill's mother, it seemed, was an avid reader of his novels and a great fan of his into the bargain.

The books said more about him than Alex would ever have been aware; there wasn't a sympathetic female character in any of them. The cuttings were even more illuminating, especially the ones with pictures of Alex and his ex-wife together. There was no denying she was beautiful, but it was a brittle, superficial kind of loveliness. Her smile in every photo was only ever for the camera, never for the husband standing beside her; and, tellingly, there was always a space between them.

Dana recognised that while they might have been in love once, from the faces in the newspaper photographs it was quite clear that any love, or even affection, had long since died between them. It would seem they had remained together as long as they did for appearances' sake only. If Alex's ex-wife ever did reappear — and it seemed unlikely in the extreme — she could have no effect on Dana's relationship with Alex.

She received another boost when a picture of Alex's agent surfaced: the pleasant-faced woman was well into her fifties, and had been married for many years into the bargain. Dana winced as she remembered that she had never actually asked Maggie about the woman's marital status, but had immediately jumped to a conclusion that was obviously totally wrong. How, she asked herself, could she really blame Alex when he did exactly the same? She had been as reluctant to trust him as he had been to trust her. Two insecure people drawn irresistibly together and then torn apart because of that very same lack of trust — Alex because of his past experiences, and she ... Dana asked herself what her problem was, and the only answer that she could come up with was, quite simply, inexperience.

Dana had never been in love — had never especially wanted to be — so when it hit her like a bolt out of the blue, she just hadn't known how to deal with it. She had been just as afraid, in her own way, as Alex had been in his. She found herself grinning wryly as she admitted that it was no wonder they had encountered so many problems.

'So . . . ' The word sounded loud in the silence of her flat. 'I want you, Alex Mitchell, and I know you want me. But . . . ' She sighed and stroked the blurred newspaper photo absently. 'How do I make you admit it? How do I convince you, once and for all, that I am not like the rest?'

★   ★   ★

In the end there seemed to be only one sensible thing that she could do. And much as the thought of facing Alex again unnerved her, Dana simply turned up on the doorstep of the Thatches on what she knew was Maggie's night off.

Alex couldn't hide his initial surprise, but he recovered with impressive speed. Dana watched as his eyes narrowed to uncompromising slits, and she suppressed a shudder.

'Well, well,' he drawled. 'What do we have here?'

Dana could only stare into Alex's face; a face devoid of any and all expression. There was nothing, nothing at all. It seemed she had taken the biggest gamble of her life — and lost.

She had been so very sure, but now she knew. Alex didn't want her. He felt nothing at all for her. She had misread all the signs, and the messages she had seen so clearly in those deep green eyes had just been wishful thinking.

What mad impulse, she asked herself in the silence that stretched between them, had led her to place herself in a position to be rejected, so finally and humiliatingly that she was left with nothing — not even her pride?

'I suggest you leave. Go back to wherever you came from.'

Had her gaze moved even for one second from his face, Dana would have missed the sudden darkening of those watchful green eyes. She would never have known the sudden, enormous surge of elation that sizzled along her veins, heating her blood to fever pitch and rocketing her confidence with sudden knowledge that refused this time to be shaken. No longer afraid to show her love, she faced him steadily, telling him almost conversationally, 'I'm not going anywhere without you. Whatever you do, whatever you say, I won't ever leave — because this is where I belong.'

He stood so still, so silent, he could have been turned to stone, his gaze never leaving her face. Then he said just one word: 'Why?'

It was almost a cry of anguish, full of fear and doubt, and Dana had never loved him more than she did at that moment. She had also never been more certain that she was doing the right thing.

'Because I love you,' she said simply. 'And I think you love me. Whatever you want in a woman, Alex, is what I will and can be.'

Still he didn't move, not so much as a muscle. Dana waited patiently, knowing it wasn't going to be easy for him to trust again, understanding that it would take time. Time that only Alex could give them, if he would.

'We got off on the wrong foot,' she continued, speaking gently, her voice low. 'It started almost as a game, the deception that I played on you. I wanted to see if I could be the secretary that you wanted where all the others had failed. But now I want to be the woman that you want — the woman you need. And I know that I can be.'

The grim face relaxed fractionally, the hard gaze softened, and Alex said quietly, 'You already are.'

Nothing came that easily. Dana knew that you had to fight for what you wanted, in business and in life, and she was prepared for that. She had misheard him; he couldn't possibly have said what she thought he had said. She quelled the rising excitement ruthlessly. 'What?'

He smiled then and took a step forward, before repeating in a stronger tone, 'You already are everything I want, everything I need — baggy-suited, mini-skirted, efficient, attractive . . . ' His voice deepened. 'I can't — I won't — fight it any longer. Anything you want to be, and everything you are, is what I want, and so much more than I deserve.'

Dana took a hesitant step and in the same instant Alex closed the gap between them, folding her into his arms with a deep sigh of pure pleasure. They stood like that for a long moment with no need of words, sure at long last of the love that had surfaced so unexpectedly between them.

'How often I wanted you in my arms like this,' he murmured against her hair. 'But even when I had you here, I could never quite believe it was where you wanted to be, or that I could persuade you to stay.'

'And I couldn't believe that love could come like that.' She lifted her head to look into his eyes. 'So suddenly, like a bolt from the blue.' She shook her head wonderingly. 'We both tried so hard to deny it, and in doing so, almost lost the greatest gift we would ever be given. I — ' The rest of what she had been going to say was lost, as Alex claimed her mouth with his own, and then pressed a finger to her lips.

'I know,' he whispered. 'And I need to say it, too.' The look shining in the clear green of his eyes turned Dana's bones to liquid. 'I love you. I have loved you for weeks, but I was just too stubborn and afraid to admit it. I've been wrong about a lot of things, and I can't get over how lucky I am that you had the patience to prove it to me. Without you . . . '

He shuddered deeply and Dana's heart went out to him, for all that he had been through and all that he might have missed — that they both might have missed — if he hadn't finally been willing to let love back into his life.

'You won't ever be without me,' she promised, meeting his gaze steadily. 'I love you more than you'll ever know, and I will never give you cause to doubt it.'